Conversational Russian Dialogues

50 RUSSIAN CONVERSATIONS TO EASILY IMPROVE YOUR VOCABULARY & BECOME FLUENT FASTER

CONVERSATIONAL RUSSIAN DUAL LANGUAGE

BOOKS VOL. 1

TOURI

https://touri.co/

ISBN: 978-1-953149-18-3

CONTENTS

FREE AUDIOBOOKS

Touri has partnered with AudiobookRocket.com!

If you love audiobooks, here is your opportunity to get the NEWEST audiobooks completely FREE!

Thrillers, Fantasy, Young Adult, Kids, African-American Fiction, Women's Fiction, Sci-Fi, Comedy, Classics and many more genres!

Visit AudiobookRocket.com!

RESOURCES

TOURI.CO

Some of the best ways to become fluent in a new language is through repetition, memorization and conversation. If you'd like to practice your newly learned vocabulary, Touri offers live fun and immersive 1-on-1 online language lessons with native instructors at nearly anytime of the day. For more information go to <u>Touri.co</u> now.

FACEBOOK GROUP
Learn Spanish - Touri Language Learning

Learn French - Touri Language Learning

YOUTUBE
Touri Language Learning Channel

ANDROID APP
Learn Spanish App for Beginners

BOOKS

SPANISH

Conversational Spanish Dialogues: 50 Spanish Conversations and Short Stories

Spanish Short Stories (Volume 1): 10 Exciting Short Stories to Easily Learn Spanish & Improve Your Vocabulary

Spanish Short Stories (Volume 2): 10 Exciting Short Stories to Easily Learn Spanish & Improve Your Vocabulary

Intermediate Spanish Short Stories (Volume 1): 10 Amazing Short Tales to Learn Spanish & Quickly Grow Your Vocabulary the Fun Way!

Intermediate Spanish Short Stories (Volume 2): 10 Amazing Short Tales to Learn Spanish & Quickly Grow Your Vocabulary the Fun Way!

100 Days of Real World Spanish: Useful Words & Phrases for All Levels to Help You Become Fluent Faster

100 Day Medical Spanish Challenge: Daily List of Relevant Medical Spanish Words & Phrases to Help You Become Fluent

FRENCH

Conversational French Dialogues: 50 French Conversations and Short Stories

French Short Stories for Beginners (Volume 1): 10 Exciting Short Stories to Easily Learn French & Improve Your Vocabulary

French Short Stories for Beginners (Volume 2): 10 Exciting Short Stories to Easily Learn French & Improve Your Vocabulary

Intermediate French Short Stories (Volume 1): 10 Amazing Short Tales to Learn French & Quickly Grow Your Vocabulary the Fun Way!

ITALIAN

Conversational Italian Dialogues: 50 Italian Conversations and Short Stories

PORTUGUESE

Conversational Portuguese Dialogues: 50 Portuguese Conversations and Short Stories

ARABIC

Conversational Arabic Dialogues: 50 Arabic Conversations and Short Stories

CHINESE

Conversational Chinese Dialogues: 50 Chinese Conversations and Short Stories

WANT THE NEXT RUSSIAN BOOK FOR FREE?

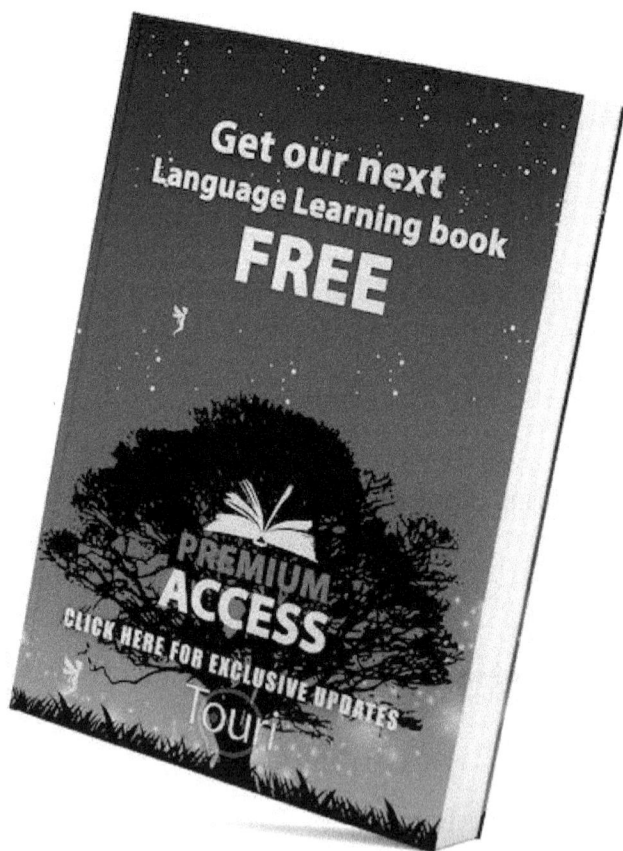

INTRODUCTION

So you're ready to take the plunge and learn Russian? What an excellent choice you have made to expand your horizons and open more doors of opportunities in your life.

If this is your first time or a continuation in your Russian learning journey, we want you to know that we're proud of you.

Did you know German is the fifth most commonly spoken language worldwide? In fact, Russian is the mother tongue for roughly 147 million people, and another 113 million speak it as a second language. Russia is also the largest country in the world – and is approximately 1.8 times the size of the US. Russian is also the official language of Belarus, Kyrgyzstan and Kazakhstan, and it's considered an unofficial lingua franca in Ukraine and many former Soviet countries. Which include Azerbaijan, Estonia, Georgia, Latvia, Lithuania, Moldova, Tajikistan, Turkmenistan and Uzbekistan.

Here's a fun fact: If you are thinking of becoming an astronaut, you have to know Russian. Nowadays, it's a requirement for NASA applicants to know the Russian language.

As you may know, learning a new language has a many benefits that expand far beyond simply navigating through a conversation with a native speaker. The ability to communicate in a foreign language will allow you to truly immerse yourself in different cultures, create more memorable travel experiences and become even more marketable for advancements in career opportunities.

It is human nature to naturally progress and learn from the day we are born. Since birth we have been shaping our preferences based on our previous experiences. These experiences have provided you important feedback about your likes, dislikes, what has made you better or worse and allowed you to learn from these lessons.

The same approach should be taken to learn a new language.

Our goal with this book is to provide engaging and fun learning material that is relevant and useful in the real Russian-speaking world. Some students are provided with difficult or boring language materials that cause the learner to become overwhelmed and give up shortly after.

Building a strong foundation of vocabulary is critical to your improvement and reaching fluency. We *guarantee* you that this book is packed with vocabulary and phrases that you can start using today.

WHAT THIS BOOK IS ABOUT & HOW IT WORKS

A sure-fire way to exponentially decrease your time to Russian fluency is to role play with key words and phrases that naturally occur in actual scenarios you experience on a daily basis.

This book has 50 examples of conversations, written in both Russian and English so you never feel lost in translation, and will ensure you boost your conversational skills quickly.

You will find each chapter different from the last as two or more characters interact in real life scenarios. You will soon learn how to ask for directions, send a package at the post office, call for help, introduce yourself and even order at a restaurant.

Sometimes a direct translation does not make sense to and from each language. Therefore, we recommend that you read each story in both languages to ensure understanding what is taking place.

Tips for Success

No doubt you can pick up this book at anytime to reference a situation that you may be in. However, in order to get the most out of this book, there is an effective approach to yield the best results.

1. **Role-play:** Learning takes place when activities are engaging and memorable. Role-play is any speaking activity when you either put yourself into someone else's shoes, or when put yourself into an imaginary situation and act it out.

2. **Look up vocab:** At some points there may be a word or phrase that you don't understand and that's completely fine. As we mentioned before, some of the translations are not word-for-word in order for the conversations to remain realistic in each language. Therefore, we recommend that you look up anything that is not fully clear to you.

3. **Create your own conversations:** After going through all of the stories we invite you to create your own by modifying what you already read. Perhaps you order additional items while at a restaurant or maybe you have an entirely different conversation over the phone. Let your imagination run wild.

4. **Seek out more dialogues:** Don't let your learning stop here. We encourage you to practice in as many ways as possible. Referencing your newly learned phrases and vocabulary, you can test your comprehension with Russian movies and television shows. Practice, practice, practice will give you the boost to fluency.

Focus on building your foundation of words and phrases commonly used in the real world and we promise your results will be staggering! Now, go out into the world, speak with confidence and in no time native speakers will be amazed by your Portguese speaking skills.

Good luck!

SURVIVAL PHRASES

1. ***Да.*** – Yes.
   Da.

2. ***Привет.*** – Hi.
   Privet.

3. ***Здравствуйте*** – Hello
   Zdravstvuyte

2. ***Доброе утро.*** – Good morning.
   Dobroe utro.

3. ***Добрый день.*** – Good afternoon.
   Dobryy den'.

4. ***Добрый вечер.*** – Good evening.
   Dobryy vecher.

5. ***Спокойной ночи.*** – Good night.
   Spokoynoy nochi.

6. ***Спасибо.*** – Thank you.
   Spasibo.

7. ***Нет*** – No
   Net.

8. ***Прошу прощения.*** – I'm sorry.
   Proshu proshcheniya.

9. ***Приятно познакомиться.*** – Nice to meet you.
   Priyatno poznakomit'sya.

10. ***Как дела?*** – How are you?
    Kak dela?

11. ***Извините.*** – Excuse me.
    Izvinite.

12. ***До свидания.*** – Goodbye.
    Do svidaniya.

13. ***Меня зовут (name).*** – I'm... (name).
    Menya zovut (name).

14. ***У меня все нормально.*** – I'm fine.
    U menya vsyo normal'no.

15. ***Большое спасибо!*** – Thank you very much
    Bol'shoye spasibo!

16. ***Пожалуйста.*** – Please.
    Pozhaluysta.

17. ***Не за что*** – You're welcome.
    Ne za chto

18. ***Как вас зовут?*** – What's your name?
    Kak vas zovut?

19. ***Откуда вы?*** – Where are you from?
    Otkuda vy?

Introducing Yourself

20. *Вы говорите по-английски / по-русски?* – Do you speak English / Russian?
    Vy gavarite pa angllyski/ pa rUsski?

21. *Да, немного* – Just a little
    Da, nimnOga

22. *Вы очень добры* – You're very kind
    vi Ochin' dabrY

23. *из Штатов / России* – I'm from the U.S / Russia
    iz ShtAtaf / Rasii

24. *Я американец* – I'm American
    yA amirikAnets

25. *Где вы живете?* – Where do you live?
    Gde vy zhivYOte?

26. *Вам здесь понравилось?* – Did you like it here?
    vAm zdEs' panrAvilas'?

27. *Чем Вы занимаетесь?* – What do you do for a living?
    Chem vy zanimAitis'?

28. *Мне нравится русский* – I like Russian
    mnE nrAvitsa Russkiy

29. *Я работаю переводчиком* – I work as a translator
    Ya rabOtayu pirivOchikam

30. *Мне нужно идти* – I have to go
    Mne nUzhna iti

31. *Я сейчас вернусь* – I will be right back
    ya sichAs virnUs'

Solving a Misunderstanding

32. **Без проблем** – No problem
    Bis prabl'Em

33. **Повторите, пожалуйста?** – Can you say it again?
    Paftarite pazhAlusta?

34. **Напишите, пожалуйста** – Write it down please
    Napichite pazhAlusta

35. **Я не понимаю** – I don't understand
    Ya ni panimAju

36. **Понятия не имею** – I have no idea
    PanyAtiya ni imEyu

37. **Как сказать "please" по-русски?** – How do you say "Please" in Russian?
    kAk skazAt' "please" parUski?

38. **Что это?** – What is this?
    chtO eta?

Words & Expressions

39. *Удачи!* – Good luck!
    udAchi!

40. *С Новым Годом!* – Happy New Year
    S nOvym gOdam!

41. *Поздравляю!* – Congratulations!
    pazdravlyAyu!

42. *Вам (это) нравится?* – Do you like it?
    Vam (eta) nrAvitsa?

43. *Я себя плохо чувствую* – I feel sick
    Ya sibyA ploha chUstvuyu

44. *Мне нужен врач* – I need a doctor
    MnE nUzhin vrAch

45. *Что это?* – What is this?
    chtO eta?

46. *Сколько сейчас времени?* – What time is it?
    Skol'ka sichAs vr'Emini?

47. *Я хочу есть* – I'm hungry
    Ya hAchu YEst'

48. *Я хочу пить* – I'm thirsty ‸
    Ya hAchu pit'

49. *Завтра* – Tomorrow
    zAftra

50. *Вчера* – Yesterday
    fchirA

1. Формальное приветствие – FORMAL''NOE PRIVETSTVIE FORMAL GREETING

Джон: Доброе утро, профессор Джастин. Как у вас дела?
Dzhon: Dobroe utro, professor Dzhastin. Kak u vas dela?

Профессор Джастин: Доброе утро, Джон. У меня все хорошо. А у вас?
Professor Dzhastin: Dobroe utro, Dzhon. U meniâ vse khorosho. A u vas?

Джон: Хорошо, спасибо. Это моя подруга Кларисса. Она думает о поступлении в этот университет. У нее есть несколько вопросов. Не могли бы вы рассказать нам о процессе, пожалуйста?
Dzhon: Xorosho, spasibo. Éto moiâ podruga Klarissa. Ona dumaet o postuplenii v étot universitet. U nee est' neskol'ko voprosov. Ne mogli by vy rasskazat' nam o protŝesse, pozhaluĭsta?

Профессор Джастин: Здравствуйте, Кларисса! Приятно с вами познакомиться. Я более чем рад поговорить с вами. Зайходите в мой офис на следующей неделе.
Professor Dzhastin: Zdravstvuĭte, Klarissa! Priiâtno s vami poznakomit'siâ. ÎA bolee chem rad pogovorit' s vami. Zaĭkhodite v moĭ ofis na sleduiûshcheĭ nedele.

Кларисса: Приятно познакомиться, профессор. Большое вам спасибо за помощь.
Klarissa: Priiâtno poznakomit'siâ, professor. Bol'shoe vam spasibo za pomoshch'.

Профессор Джастин: Конечно. Надеюсь, я смогу ответить на ваши вопросы!
Professor Dzhastin: Konechno. Nadeiûs', iâ smogu otvetit' na vashi voprosy!

FORMAL GREETING

John: Good morning, Professor Justin, how are you doing?

Professor Justin: Good morning, John. I am doing well. And you?

John: I'm well, thank you. This is my friend Clarissa. She is thinking about applying to this university. She has a few questions. Would you mind telling us about the process, please?

Professor Justin: Hello, Clarissa! It's a pleasure to meet you. I'm more than happy to speak with you. Please stop by my office next week.

Clarissa: It's a pleasure to meet you, professor. Thank you so much for helping us.

Professor Justin: Of course. Hopefully, I will be able to answer your questions!

2. НЕФОРМАЛЬНОЕ ПРИВЕТСТВИЕ – NEFORMAL''NOE PRIVETSTVIE
INFORMAL GREETING

Джеф: Кто та высокая женщина рядом с Барбарой?
Dzhef: Kto ta vysokai͡a zhenshchina ri͡adom s Barbaroĭ?

Чарльз: Это ее подруга Мэри. Ты разве не знакомился с ней на вечеринке у Стива?
CHarl'z: Ėto ee podruga Mėri. Ty razve ne znakomilsi͡a s neĭ na vecherinke u Stiva?

Джеф: Нет, я не был у Стива на вечеринке.
Dzhef: Net, i͡a ne byl u Stiva na vecherinke.

Чарльз: Ну так давай я познакомлю вас сейчас. Мэри, это мой друг Джеф.
CHarl'z: Nu tak davaĭ i͡a poznakomli͡u vas seĭchas. Mėri, ėto moĭ drug Dzhef.

Мэри: Привет, Джеф. Приятно познакомиться.
Mėri: Privet, Dzhef. Prii͡atno poznakomit'si͡a.

Джеф: Мне тоже. Что-нибудь хочешь выпить,
Dzhef: Mne tozhe. CHto-nibud' khochesh' vypit',

Мэри: Да, конечно. Давай возьмем что-нибудь.
Mėri: Da, konechno. Davaĭ voz'mem chto-nibud'.

INFORMAL GREETING

Jeff: Who's the tall woman next to Barbara?

Charles: That's her friend Mary. Didn't you meet her at Steve's party?

Jeff: No, I wasn't at Steve's party.

Charles: Oh! Then let me introduce you to her now. Mary, this is my friend Jeff.

Mary: Hi, Jeff. Nice to meet you.

Jeff: You, too. Would you like a drink?

Mary: Sure, let's go get one.

3. ТЕЛЕФОННЫЙ ЗВОНОК – TELEFONNYĬ ZVONOK A TELEPHONE CALL

Джон: Привет, Элис. Это Джон. Как дела?
Dzhon: Privet, Élis. Éto Dzhon. Kak dela?

Элис: О, Джон, привет! Как раз вспоминала о тебе.
Élis: O, Dzhon, privet! Kak raz vspominala o tebe.

Джон: Классно. Слушай, а ты не хочешь со мной сходить в кино вечером?
Dzhon: Klassno. Slushaĭ, a ty ne khochesh' so mnoĭ skhodit' v kino vecherom?

Элис: Конечно, очень! А на какой фильм ты хочешь сходить?
Élis: Konechno, ochen'! A na kakoĭ fil'm ty khochesh' skhodit'?

Джон: Я подумал, может, на новую комедию *Тушите свет*. Как тебе идея?
Dzhon: ĪA podumal, mozhet, na novuiu̯ komediiu̯ Tushite svet. Kak tebe ideĭa?

Элис: Отличная идея.
Élis: Otlichnaĭa ideĭa.

Джон: Окей, тогда я заеду за тобой в половине восьмого. Фильм начинается в 8.
Dzhon: Okeĭ, togda ĭa zaedu za toboĭ v polovine vos'mogo. Fil'm nachinaetsĭa v 8.

Элис: Ладно, до встречи. Пока.
Élis: Ladno, do vstrechi. Poka.

A TELEPHONE CALL

John: Hi, Alice, it's John. How are you?

Alice: Oh, hi, John! I was just thinking about you.

John: That's nice. I was wondering if you'd like to go to a movie tonight.

Alice: Sure, I'd love to! Which movie do you want to see?

John: I was thinking about that new comedy *Turn Off the Lights.* What do you think?

Alice: Sounds great!

John: Ok, I'll pick you up around 7:30. The movie starts at 8:00.

Alice: See you then. Bye!

4. Который Час? – KOTORYĬ CHAS?
WHAT TIME IS IT?

Наташа: Который час? Мы опаздываем!
Natasha: Kotoryĭ chas? My opazdyvaem!

Тони: Пятнадцать минут восьмого. Мы как раз успеваем. Не паникуй.
Toni: P͡iatnadt͡sat' minut vos'mogo. My kak raz uspevaem. Ne panikuĭ.

Наташа: Я думала, что мы должны быть в ресторане к половине восьмого, чтобы быть вовремя на вечеринке-сюрпризе. А с таким вечерним движением мы вряд ли успеем.
Natasha: I͡A dumala, chto my dolzhny byt' v restorane k polovine vos'mogo, chtoby byt' vovrem͡ia na vecherinke-s͡iurprize. A s takim vechernim dvizheniem my vr͡iad li uspeem.

Тони: Я уверен, что мы будем там вовремя. Час-пик уже почти прошел. Во всяком случае, вечеринка начинается в восемь. Сейчас мне нужна помощь по поводу проезда. Позвони, пожалуйста, в ресторан и узнай, куда нам припарковать машину.
Toni: I͡A uveren, chto my budem tam vovrem͡ia. CHas-pik uzhe pochti proshel. Vo vs͡iakom sluchae, vecherinka nachinaets͡ia v vosem'. Seĭchas mne nuzhna pomoshch' po povodu proezda. Pozvoni, pozhaluĭsta, v restoran i uznaĭ, kuda nam priparkovat' mashinu.

Наташа: Без проблем.
Natasha: Bez problem.

WHAT TIME IS IT?

Natasha: What time is it? We're going to be late!

Tony: It's a quarter after seven. We're on time. Don't panic.

Natasha: But I thought we had to be at the restaurant by 7:30 for the surprise party. We'll never make it there with all this evening traffic.

Tony: I'm sure we will. Rush hour is almost over. Anyway, the party starts at 8:00. But I do need help with directions. Can you call the restaurant and ask them where we park our car?

Natasha: Of course.

5. Повтори, пожалуйста – POVTORI, POZHALUĬSTA
CAN YOU SAY THAT AGAIN?

Люк: Алло! Привет, Стефани. Как там дела в офисе?
Lĭuk: Allo! Privet, Stefani. Kak tam dela v ofise?

Стефани: Привет, Люк? Как ты? Ты можешь заехать в магазин и купить еще бумаги для принтера?
Stefani: Privet, Lĭuk? Kak ty? Ty mozhesh' zaekhat' v magazin i kupit' eshche bumagi dlĩa printera?

Люк: Что ты говоришь? Повтори, пожалуйста. Ты имеешь в виду купить чернила для принтера? Прости, связь плохая.
Lĭuk: CHto ty govorish'? Povtori, pozhaluĭsta. Ty imeesh' v vidu kupit' chernila dlĩa printera? Prosti, sviãz' plokhaĩa.

Стефани: А сейчас слышно? Нет, мне нужна еще бумага для компьютера. Слушай, я тебе сообщением пришлю точно, что мне нужно. Спасибо, Люк. Поговорим позже.
Stefani: A seĭchas slyshno? Net, mne nuzhna eshche bumaga dlĩa komp'ĩutera. Slushaĭ, ĩa tebe soobshcheniem prishlĩu tochno, chto mne nuzhno. Spasibo, Lĭuk. Pogovorim pozzhe.

Люк: Спасибо, Стефани. Извини, у меня здесь реально очень плохо ловит телефон.
Lĭuk: Spasibo, Stefani. Izvini, u menĩa zdes' real'no ochen' plokho lovit telefon.

24

CAN YOU SAY THAT AGAIN?

Luke: Hello? Hi, Stephanie, how are things at the office?

Stephanie: Hi, Luke! How are you? Can you please stop at the store and pick up extra paper for the printer?

Luke: What did you say? Can you repeat that, please? Did you say to pick up ink for the printer? Sorry, the phone is cutting out.

Stephanie: Can you hear me now? No, I need more computer paper. Listen, I'll text you exactly what I need. Thanks, Luke.

Talk to you later.

Luke: Thanks, Stephanie. Sorry, my phone has really bad reception here.

6. Совпадения – SOVPADENIIA
COINCIDENCES

Мэг: Привет, Джулия! Давно не виделись!
Mėg: Privet, Dzhuliia! Davno ne videlis'!

Джулия: Мэг! Привет! Мы с тобой не виделись целую вечность. Вот это случайность! Что ты здесь делаешь?
Dzhuliia: Mėg! Privet! My s toboĭ ne videlis' tseluiu vechnost'. Vot ėto sluchaĭnost'! CHto ty zdes' delaesh'?

Мэг: Я получила новую работу в центре города, вот покупаю себе одежду. Кстати, как тебе эта рубашка?
Mėg: IA poluchila novuiu rabotu v tsentre goroda, vot pokupaiu sebe odezhdu. Kstati, kak tebe ėta rubashka?

Джулия: Мммм…Ты же знаешь, как я люблю синий цвет. Понимаешь… у меня такая же рубашка.
Dzhuliia: Mmmm…Ty zhe znaesh', kak ia liubliu siniĭ tsvet. Ponimaesh'… u menia takaia zhe rubashka.

Мэг: У тебя всегда был хороший вкус. Как же тесен мир!
Mėg: U tebia vsegda byl khoroshiĭ vkus. Kak zhe tesen mir!

COINCIDENCES

Meg: Well, hello there, Julia! Long time no see!

Julia: Meg! Hi! What a coincidence! I haven't seen you in forever! What are you doing here?

Meg: I just got a new job in the city, so I'm shopping for some clothes. Hey, what do you think of this shirt?

Julia: Hmmm… Well, you know how much I love blue. See? I've got the same shirt!

Meg: You always did have good taste! What a small world.

7. Погода – POGODA
THE WEATHER

Сэлли: На улице очень холодно! Что там с прогнозом погоды? Я думала, что холодный фронт должен был уже пройти.
Sélli: Na ulit͡se ochen' kholodno! CHto tam s prognozom pogody? I͡A dumala, chto kholodnyĭ front dolzhen byl uzhe proĭti.

Габриела: Ну да, я тоже. Я как раз об этом сегодня утром и читала онлайн.
Gabriela: Nu da, i͡a tozhe. I͡A kak raz ob étom segodni͡a utrom i chitala onlaĭn.

Сэлли: Мне кажется, холодный ветер точно понижает температуру воздуха.
Sélli: Mne kazhetsi͡a, kholodnyĭ veter tochno ponizhaet temperaturu vozdukha.

Габриела: Давай зайдем внутрь. Я чувствую, что мои пальцы на ногах начинают неметь.
Gabriela: Davaĭ zaĭdem vnutr'. I͡A chuvstvui͡u, chto moi pal't͡sy na nogakh nachinai͡ut nemet'.

THE WEATHER

Sally: It's freezing outside! What happened to the weather report? I thought this cold front was supposed to pass.

Gabriela: Yeah, I thought so too. That's what I read online this morning.

Sally: I guess the wind chill is really driving down the temperature.

Gabriela: Can we go inside? I feel like my toes are starting to go numb.

8. Заказ еды – ZAKAZ EDY
ORDERING FOOD

Официант: Здравствуйте. Сегодня я буду вашим официантом. Желаете для начала что-нибудь выпить?
Ofitsiant: Zdravstvuĭte. Segodnia ia budu vashim ofitsiantom. ZHelaete dlia nachala chto-nibud' vypit'?

Шон: Да, мне бы чая со льдом, пожалуйста.
SHon: Da, mne by chaia so l'dom, pozhaluĭsta.

Анна: А мне лимонад, пожалуйста.
Anna: A mne limonad, pozhaluĭsta.

Официант: Отлично. Вы уже готовы заказывать или вам нужно несколько минут?
Ofitsiant: Otlichno. Vy uzhe gotovy zakazyvat' ili vam nuzhno neskol'ko minut?

Шон: Мы, пожалуй, готовы. Для начала я возьму томатный суп и ростбиф с картофельным пюре и горошком.
SHon: My, pozhaluĭ, gotovy. Dlia nachala ia voz'mu tomatnyĭ sup i rostbif s kartofel'nym piure i goroshkom.

Официант: Как вам приготовить ростбиф – слабо прожаренный, средний или хорошо прожаренный?
Ofitsiant: Kak vam prigotovit' rostbif – slabo prozharennyĭ, sredniĭ ili khorosho prozharennyĭ?

Шон: Хорошо прожаренный
SHon: Xorosho prozharennyĭ

Анна: А я буду рыбу с картошкой и салатом.
Anna: A ia budu rybu s kartoshkoĭ i salatom.

ORDERING FOOD

Waiter: Hello, I'll be your waiter today. Can I start you off with something to drink?

Sean: Yes. I would like iced tea, please.

Anna: And I'll have lemonade., please.

Waiter: Ok. Are you ready to order, or do you need a few minutes?

Sean: I think we're ready. I'll have the tomato soup to start, and the roast beef with mashed potatoes and peas.

Waiter: How do you want the beef — rare, medium, or well done?

Sean: Well done, please.

Anna: And I'll just have the fish, with potatoes and a salad.

9. ВИЗИТ К ВРАЧУ – VIZIT K VRACHU
VISITING THE DOCTOR

Доктор: Какая у вас проблема?
Doktor: Kakai͡a u vas problema?

Кэти: Ну, у меня сильный кашель и болит горло. Еще у меня болит голова.
Kėti: Nu, u meni͡a sil'nyĭ kashel' i bolit gorlo. Eshche u meni͡a bolit golova.

Доктор: Как долго у вас эти симптомы?
Doktor: Kak dolgo u vas ėti simptomy?

Кэти: Уже около трех дней. И еще я чувствую сильную усталость.
Kėti: Uzhe okolo trekh dneĭ. I eshche i͡a chuvstvui͡u sil'nui͡u ustalost'.

Доктор: Хмм. Похоже, у вас грипп. Принимайте аспирин каждые четыре часа и много отдыхайте. Обязательно пейте много жидкости. Если на следующей неделе вы все еще будете болеть, позвоните мне.
Doktor: Xmm. Pokhozhe, u vas gripp. Prinimaĭte aspirin kazhdye chetyre chasa i mnogo otdykhaĭte. Obi͡azatel'no peĭte mnogo zhidkosti. Esli na sledui͡ushcheĭ nedele vy vse eshche budete bolet', pozvonite mne.

Кэти: Хорошо, спасибо.
Kėti: Xorosho, spasibo.

VISITING THE DOCTOR

Doctor: What seems to be the problem?

Cathy: Well... I have a bad cough and a sore throat. I also have a headache.

Doctor: How long have you had these symptoms?

Cathy: About three days now. And I'm really tired, too.

Doctor: Hmm. It sounds like you've got the flu. Take aspirin every four hours and get plenty of rest. Make sure you drink lots of fluids. Call me if you're still sick next week.

Cathy: Ok, thank you.

10.   Как пройти / проехать – Kak proyti / proyekhat'
Asking For Directions

Марк: Простите, не подскажете, где библиотека?
Mark: Prostite, ne podskazhete, gde biblioteka?

Оливия: Да, подскажу. В эту сторону. Идете три квартала до Вашингтон стрит и поворачиваете налево. Она на углу, напротив банка.
Oliviîa: Da, podskazhu. V ètu storonu. Idete tri kvartala do Vashington strit i povorachivaete nalevo. Ona na uglu, naprotiv banka.

Марк: Спасибо! В городе всего только три дня, поэтому совсем еще не ориентируюсь, где что находится.
Mark: Spasibo! V gorode vsego tol'ko tri dnîa, poétomu sovsem eshche ne orientiruîus', gde chto nakhoditsîa.

Оливия: Понимаю вас. Мы сами переехали сюда год назад.и до сих пор не совсем знаем, где и что находится.
Oliviîa: Ponimaîu vas. My sami pereekhali sîuda god nazad.i do sikh por ne sovsem znaem, gde i chto nakhoditsîa.

ASKING FOR DIRECTIONS

Marc: Excuse me. Could you tell me where the library is?

Olivia: Yes, it's that way. You go three blocks to Washington Street, then turn right. It's on the corner, across from the bank.

Marc: Thanks! I've only been in town a few days, so I really don't know my way around yet.

Olivia: Oh, I know how you feel. We moved here a year ago, and I still don't know where everything is!

11. ЗВОНОК О ПОМОЩИ – ZVONOK O POMOSHCHI
CALLING FOR HELP

Питер: Представляешь, эта машина просто проскочила на красный свет и сбила этот грузовик!
Piter: Predstavlĩaesh', ėta mashina prosto proskochila na krasnyĭ svet i sbila ėtot gruzovik!

Гейл: Кто-нибудь пострадал?
Geĭl: Kto-nibud' postradal?

Питер: Я не знаю ... давай позвоним 911. ... Здравствуйте! Я хотел бы сообщить об автомобильной аварии возле почтового отделения на Хьюстон-стрит. Похоже, человеку больно. Да, это просто случилось. Хорошо спасибо. До свидания.
Piter: ĨA ne znaĩu ... davaĭ pozvonim 911. ... Zdravstvuĭte! ĨA khotel by soobshchit' ob avtomobil'noĭ avarii vozle pochtovogo otdelenĩia na X'ĩuston-strit. Pokhozhe, cheloveku bol'no. Da, ėto prosto sluchilos'. Xorosho spasibo. Do svidanĩia.

Гейл: Что они сказали?
Geĭl: CHto oni skazali?

Питер: Они немедленно отправят скорую помощь и полицейскую машину.
Piter: Oni nemedlenno otpravĩat skoruĩu pomoshch' i politseĭskuĩu mashinu.

Гейл: Ну вот, они здесь. Я надеюсь, что с человеком все в порядке.
Geĭl: Nu vot, oni zdes'. ĨA nadeĩus', chto s chelovekom vse v porĩadke.

Питер: Да. Надо быть очень осторожным, когда водишь машину.
Piter: Da. Nado byt' ochen' ostorozhnym, kogda vodish' mashinu.

CALLING FOR HELP

Peter: Hey! That car just ran a red light and hit that truck!

Gail: Is anyone hurt?

Peter: I don't know... let's call 911. ...Hello? I'd like to report a car accident near the post office on Houston Street. It looks like a man is hurt. Yes, it just happened. Ok, thanks. Bye.

Gail: What did they say?

Peter: They're going to send an ambulance and a police car right away.

Gail: Good, they're here. I hope the man is alright.

Peter: I know. You have to be so careful when you're driving.

12. ЗА ПОКУПКАМИ – ZA POKUPKAMI
SHOPPING

Луиз: Слушай, Джулия…Взгляни на эти десерты! Может, напечем печенья сегодня?
Luiz: Slushaĭ, Dzhuliĭa…Vzglĭani na éti deserty! Mozhet, napechem pechen'ĭa segodnĭa?

Джулия: Хмм. Классная идея! Раз уж мы здесь, давай наберем ингредиентов.
Dzhuliĭa: Xmm. Klassnaĭa ideĭa! Raz uzh my zdes', davaĭ naberem ingredientov.

Луиз: Ладно. Что нам нужно?
Luiz: Ladno. CHto nam nuzhno?

Джулия: В рецепте мука, сахар и сливочное масло. Ой, нам еще нужны яйца и шоколадная стружка.
Dzhuliĭa: V retsepte muka, sakhar i slivochnoe maslo. Oĭ, nam eshche nuzhny ĭaĭtsa i shokoladnaĭa struzhka.

Луиз: Почему бы не взять молочное? Они в холодильном отделе в дальней части магазина. Я наберу сухих ингредиентов. По-моему, они в 10-м ряду.
Luiz: Pochemu by ne vzĭat' molochnoe? Oni v kholodil'nom otdele v dal'neĭ chasti magazina. ĬA naberu sukhikh ingredientov. Po-moemu, oni v 10-m rĭadu.

Джулия: Отлично! Давай встретимся у кассы.
Dzhuliĭa: Otlichno! Davaĭ vstretimsĭa u kassy.

Луиз: Хорошо, встречаемся там.
Luiz: Xorosho, vstrechaemsĭa tam.

SHOPPING

Louise: Hey, Julia... Look at those desserts! How about baking some cookies today?

Julia: Hmm... Yeah, that's a great idea! While we're here, let's pick up the ingredients.

Julia: Ok, what do we need?

Louise: The recipe calls for flour, sugar and butter. Oh, and we also need eggs and chocolate chips.

Julia: Why don't you get the dairy ingredients? You'll find those in the refrigerated section in the back of the store. I'll get the dry ingredients. I believe they're in aisle 10.

Louise: Great! Let's meet at the checkout.

Julia: Ok. See you there.

13. БЕГАТЬ ПО ДЕЛАМ – BEGAT'' PO DELAM
RUNNING ERRANDS

Администратор отеля: Здравствуйте. Чем могу вам помочь?
Administrator otelia: Zdravstvuĭte. CHem mogu vam pomoch'?

Клэр: Ну, я в городе всего на несколько дней, и мне нужно кое-что сделать, пока я здесь.
Klėr: Nu, ia v gorode vsego na neskol'ko dneĭ, i mne nuzhno koe-chto sdelat', poka ia zdes'.

Администратор отеля: Конечно. Что вам нужно сделать?
Administrator otelia: Konechno. CHto vam nuzhno sdelat'?

Клэр: Я хочу сделать себе стрижку. И мне еще нужно подшить мои новые брюки.
Klėr: IA khochu sdelat' sebe strizhku. I mne eshche nuzhno podshit' moi novye briuki.

Администратор отеля: Ясно. Вот вам карта города. Вот здесь есть хороший салон, и он находится всего в квартале отсюда. Там же есть портной. Что-нибудь еще?
Administrator otelia: IAsno. Vot vam karta goroda. Vot zdes' est' khoroshiĭ salon, i on nakhoditsia vsego v kvartale otsiuda. Tam zhe est' portnoĭ. CHto-nibud' eshche?

Клэр: Да. Мне нужно будет проверить машину перед длительной поездкой домой!
Klėr: Da. Mne nuzhno budet proverit' mashinu pered dlitel'noĭ poezdkoĭ domoĭ!

Администратор отеля: Конечно, без проблем. В нескольких кварталах отсюда есть хороший сервис.
Administrator otelia: Konechno, bez problem. V neskol'kikh kvartalakh otsiuda est' khoroshiĭ servis.

RUNNING ERRANDS

Hotel receptionist: Hello there. How can I help you?

Claire: Well, I'm in town visiting for a few days, and I need to get some things done while I'm here.

Hotel receptionist: Sure. What do you need?

Claire: I need to get my hair cut. I also need to have my new pants hemmed.

Hotel receptionist: Ok. Here's a map of the city. There's a good hair salon here, which is just a block away. And there's a tailor right here. Is there anything else?

Claire: Yes. I'll need to get my car serviced before my long drive back home!

Hotel receptionist: No problem. There's a good mechanic a few blocks away.

14. НА ПОЧТЕ – NA POCHTE
AT THE POST OFFICE

Работник почты: Чем могу вам помочь?
Rabotnik pochty: CHem mogu vam pomoch'?

Кэрол: Мне нужно отправить этот пакет в Нью Йорк.
Kȇrol: Mne nuzhno otpravit' ėtot paket v N'i͡u Ĭork.

Работник почты: Хорошо, давайте его взвесим...примерно 2кг 200 граммов. Если вы воспользуетесь экспресс-услугой, он доедет туда завтра. Если воспользуетесь приоритетной услугой, посылка будет доставлена в субботу.
Rabotnik pochty: Xorosho, davaĭte ego vzvesim...primerno 2kg 200 grammov. Esli vy vospol'zuetes' ėkspress-uslugoĭ, on doedet tuda zavtra. Esli vospol'zuetes' prioritetnoĭ uslugoĭ, posylka budet dostavlena v subbotu.

Кэрол: В субботу меня устраивает. Сколько это будет стоить?
Kȇrol: V subbotu meni͡a ustraivaet. Skol'ko ėto budet stoit'?

Работник почты: $12.41. Что-нибудь еще?
Rabotnik pochty: $12.41. CHto-nibud' eshche?

Кэрол: о, да! Чуть не забыла. Мне еще нужен альбом марок.
Kȇrol: o, da! CHut' ne zabyla. Mne eshche nuzhen al'bom marok.

Работник почты: Итого получается $18.94.
Rabotnik pochty: Itogo poluchaetsi͡a $18.94.

AT THE POST OFFICE

Postal clerk: How can I help you today?

Carol: I need to mail this package to New York, please.

Postal clerk: Ok, let's see how much it weighs... it's about five pounds. If you send it express, it will get there tomorrow. Or you can send it priority and it will get there by Saturday.

Carol: Saturday is fine. How much will that be?

Postal clerk: $12.41. Do you need anything else?

Carol: Oh, yeah! I almost forgot. I need a book of stamps, too.

Postal clerk: Ok, your total comes to $18.94.

15. ЭКЗАМЕН – ĖKZAMEN
THE EXAM

Шерил: Привет! Как прошел экзамен по физике?
SHeril: Privet! Kak proshel ėkzamen po fizike?

Фрэнк: Спасибо, нормально. Я так рад, что он закончился! А твоя...как твоя презентация прошла?
Frėnk: Spasibo, normal'no. ÎA tak rad, chto on zakonchilsîa! A tvoîa...kak tvoîa prezentaţsiîa proshla?

Шерил: Отлично прошла. Спасибо, что помог мне!
SHeril: Otlichno proshla. Spasibo, chto pomog mne!

Фрэнк: Да все нормально. Ну что, есть желание завтра позаниматься математикой – подготовиться к экзамену?
Frėnk: Da vse normal'no. Nu chto, est' zhelanie zavtra pozanimat'sîa matematikoĭ – podgotovit'sîa k ėkzamenu?

Шерил: Да, конечно! Приходи завтра примерно в 10 после завтрака.
SHeril: Da, konechno! Prikhodi zavtra primerno v 10 posle zavtraka.

Фрэнк: Ладно. Я принесу все свои записи.
Frėnk: Ladno. ÎA prinesu vse svoi zapisi.

THE EXAM

Cheryl: Hey! How did your physics exam go?

Frank: Not bad, thanks. I'm just glad it's over! How about your... how'd your presentation go?

Cheryl: Oh, it went really well. Thanks for helping me with it!

Frank: No problem. So... do you feel like studying tomorrow for our math exam?

Cheryl: Yeah, sure! Come over around 10:00 am, after breakfast.

Frank: All right. I'll bring my notes.

16. Отличный свитер – Otlichnyĭ sviter
The Perfect Sweater

Продавец: Вам помочь?
Prodavets: Vam pomoch'?

Глория: Да. Я ищу свитер среднего размера М.
Gloriia: Da. ÍA ishchu sviter srednego razmera M.

Продавец: Давайте посмотрим...вот симпатичный белый свитер. Как вам он?
Prodavets: Davaĭte posmotrim...vot simpatichnyĭ belyĭ sviter. Kak vam on?

Глория: Я думаю, мне бы больше подошел такой же синего цвета.
Gloriia: ÍA dumaiu, mne by bol'she podoshel takoĭ zhe sinego tsveta.

Продавец: Вот синий свитер размера М. Хотите примерить?
Prodavets: Vot siniĭ sviter razmera M. Xotite primerit'?

Глория: Да, он мне очень нравится. И сидит отлично. Сколько он стоит?
Gloriia: Da, on mne ochen' nravitsia. I sidit otlichno. Skol'ko on stoit?

Продавец: $41, а с налогом будет $50.
Prodavets: $41, a s nalogom budet $50.

Глория: Отлично! Я беру его. Спасибо!
Gloriia: Otlichno! ÍA beru ego. Spasibo!

THE PERFECT SWEATER

Salesperson: Can I help you?

Gloria: Yes, I'm looking for a sweater — in a size medium.

Salesperson: Let's see… here's a nice white one. What do you think?

Gloria: I think I'd rather have it in blue.

Salesperson: Ok … here's blue, in a medium. Would you

like to try it on?

Gloria: Ok … yes, I love it. It fits perfectly. How much is it?

Salesperson: It's $41. It will be $50, with tax.

Gloria: Perfect! I'll take it. Thank you!

17. Такси или автобус – Taksi ili avtobus
Taxi or Bus

Джойс: Поедем в кино на такси или на автобусе?
Dzhoĭs: Poedem v kino na taksi ili na avtobuse?

Билл: Давай на автобусе. В час пик невозможно поймать такси.
Bill: Davaĭ na avtobuse. V chas pik nevozmozhno poĭmat' taksi.

Джойс: А вон там не автобусная остановка?
Dzhoĭs: A von tam ne avtobusnai͡a ostanovka?

Билл: Да... Ой! А вот и автобус. Нужно будет бежать, чтобы успеть.
Bill: Da... Oĭ! A vot i avtobus. Nuzhno budet bezhat', chtoby uspet'.

Джойс: О, нет! Мы опоздали!
Dzhoĭs: O, net! My opozdali!

Билл: Ничего страшного. Следующий будет через 10 минут.
Bill: Nichego strashnogo. Sledui͡ushchiĭ budet cherez 10 minut.

TAXI OR BUS

Joyce: Should we take a taxi or a bus to the movie theater?

Bill: Let's take a bus. It's impossible to get a taxi during rush hour.

Joyce: Isn't that a bus stop over there?

Bill: Yes... Oh! There's a bus now. We'll have to run to catch it.

Joyce: Oh, no! We just missed it.

Bill: No problem. There'll be another one in 10 minutes.

18. Сколько вам лет? – SKOL''KO VAM LET?
How Old Are You?

Глория: Я не могу дождаться вечеринки-сюрприза по случаю дня рождения тети Мэри сегодня! А ты?
Gloriia: I͡A ne mogu dozhdat'si͡a vecherinki-si͡urpriza po sluchai͡u dni͡a rozhdenii͡a teti Méri segodni͡a! A ty?

Надя: И я тоже! Сколько ей исполняется?
Nadi͡a: I i͡a tozhe! Skol'ko eĭ ispolni͡aetsi͡a?

Глория: 5 мая ей исполнится 55.
Gloriia: 5 mai͡a eĭ ispolnitsi͡a 55.

Надя: Ничего себе! Я и не знала, что моя мама старше - ей 9 октября исполнится 58 лет. В любом случае, тетя Мэри будет очень удивлена, когда увидит нас всех здесь!
Nadi͡a: Nichego sebe! I͡A i ne znala, chto moi͡a mama starshe - eĭ 9 okti͡abri͡a ispolnitsi͡a 58 let. V li͡ubom sluchae, teti͡a Méri budet ochen' udivlena, kogda uvidit nas vsekh zdes'!

Глория: Это точно! Но нам еще нужно успеть разложить всю еду перед ее приходом ... Отлично! Теперь мы уже все готовы. Тише! Она здесь!
Gloriia: Éto tochno! No nam eshche nuzhno uspet' razlozhit' vsi͡u edu pered ee prikhodom ... Otlichno! Teper' my uzhe vse gotovy. Tishe! Ona zdes'!

Все: Сюрприз!
Vse: Si͡urpriz!

HOW OLD ARE YOU?

Gloria: I'm really excited for Aunt Mary's surprise birthday party this afternoon! Aren't you?

Nadia: Yeah! How old is she?

Gloria: She'll be 55 on May 5.

Nadia: Wow! I didn't know that my mom was older — she's going to be 58 on October 9. Anyway, Aunt Mary's going to be so surprised to see us all here!

Gloria: I know! But we still have to get all the food set up before she gets here ... Ok! We're all ready now. Shh! She's here!

All: Surprise!

19. В ТЕАТРЕ – V TEATRE
AT THE THEATER

Боб: Нам два билета на 15:30, пожалуйста.
Bob: Nam dva bileta na 15:30, pozhaluǐsta.

Билетер: Вот, пожалуйста. Приятного просмотра фильма!
Bileter: Vot, pozhaluǐsta. Pri͡atnogo prosmotra fil'ma!

[В зале]
[V zale]

Боб: Можно вас попросить подвинуться на одно место, чтобы мы с другом могли сидеть вместе?
Bob: Mozhno vas poprosit' podvinut's͡ia na odno mesto, chtoby my s drugom mogli sidet' vmeste?

Женщина: Конечно, без проблем.
ZHenshchina: Konechno, bez problem.

Боб: Большое спасибо.
Bob: Bol'shoe spasibo.

AT THE THEATER

Bob: We'd like two tickets for the 3:30 show, please.

Ticket sales: Here you go. Enjoy the movie!

[Inside the theater]

Bob: Would you mind moving over one, so my friend and I can sit together?

Woman: No, not at all.

Bob: Thank you so much!

20. ЧТО ВЫ УМЕЕТЕ ДЕЛАТЬ? – CHTO VY UMEETE DELAT''?
WHAT ARE YOU GOOD AT DOING?

Сандра: Ну...что будем делать?
Sandra: Nu...chto budem delat'?

Джули: Я люблю делать что-то своими руками и я очень хорошо рисую. Что думаешь?
Dzhuli: ÎA lîublîu delat' chto-to svoimi rukami i îa ochen' khorosho risuîu. CHto dumaesh'?

Сандра:Хмм... Может, поиграем в настольную игру? Это интереснее.
Sandra:Xmm... Mozhet, poigraem v nastol'nuîu igru? Èto interesnee.

Джули: Ладно. Давай поиграем в слова! У меня и правописание очень хорошее!
Dzhuli: Ladno. Davaĭ poigraem v slova! U menîa i pravopisanie ochen' khoroshee!

Сандра: Правда? Ну, посмотрим!
Sandra: Pravda? Nu, posmotrim!

WHAT ARE YOU GOOD AT DOING?

Sandra: So ... what should we do?

Julie: Well, I like to do arts and crafts, and I'm really good at drawing. What do you think?

Sandra: Hmm ... how about playing a board game? That would be more fun.

Julie: Ok. Let's play Scrabble! I'm really good at spelling, too!

Sandra: Oh, yeah? We'll see about that!

21. КАКОЙ ТВОЙ ЛЮБИМЫЙ ВИД СПОРТА? – KAKOĬ TVOĬ LĨUBIMYĬ VID SPORTA? **What Is Your Favorite Sport?**

Фил: Во сколько будут показывать футбол? Я думал, он начался в 12
Fil: Vo skol'ko budut pokazyvat' futbol? ĨA dumal, on nachalsĩa v 12

Джек: Наверное, у нас неправильное время. Ну, ладно…в любом случае, футбол не мой любимый спорт. Мне больше нравится баскетбол.
Dzhek: Navernoe, u nas nepravil'noe vremĩa. Nu, ladno…v lĩubom sluchae, futbol ne moĭ lĩubimyĭ sport. Mne bol'she nravitsĩa basketbol.

Фил: Правда? Я думал, твой любимый спорт это теннис! Я тоже большой фанат баскетбола.
Fil: Pravda? ĨA dumal, tvoĭ lĩubimyĭ sport éto tennis! ĨA tozhe bol'shoĭ fanat basketbola.

Джек: Может, сыграем как-нибудь?
Dzhek: Mozhet, sygraem kak-nibud'?

Фил: Конечно! Может, пойдем немного покидаем мячи в кольцо, пока футбол не начался?
Fil: Konechno! Mozhet, poĭdem nemnogo pokidaem mĩachi v kol'tso, poka futbol ne nachalsĩa?

Джек: Отличная идея. Пойдем.
Dzhek: Otlichnaĩa ideĩa. Poĭdem.

WHAT IS YOUR FAVORITE SPORT?

Phil: What time is that soccer game on? I thought it started at noon.

Jack: We must have had the wrong time. Oh, well ... soccer's not my favorite sport anyway. I much prefer basketball.

Phil: Oh, really? I thought your favorite sport was tennis! I'm a big fan of basketball, too.

Jack: How about a game sometime?

Phil: Sure thing! Why don't we go shoot some hoops now since the soccer game isn't on?

Jack: Excellent idea. Let's go.

22. ПОХОД НА МЮЗИКЛ – POXOD NA MĨUZIKL
GOING TO SEE A MUSICAL

Шеннон: Какое шикарное исполнение! Спасибо тебе, что пригласила меня на мюзикл.
SHennon: Kakoe shikarnoe ispolnenie! Spasibo tebe, chto priglasila menĩa na mĩuzikl.

Елена: Пожалуйста. Я рада, что тебе понравилось представление. Хореография танцоров была необыкновенной. Напоминает мне о том далеком времени, когда я сама танцевала.
Elena: Pozhaluĭsta. ĨA rada, chto tebe ponravilos' predstavlenie. Xoreografiĩa tanŝsorov byla neobyknovennoĭ. Napominaet mne o tom dalekom vremeni, kogda ĩa sama tanŝsevala.

Шеннон: Ну, да! Ты была очень талантливой балериной. Ты скучаешь по танцам?
SHennon: Nu, da! Ty byla ochen' talantlivoĭ balerinoĭ. Ty skuchaesh' po tanŝsam?

Елена: Спасибо за комплимент, очень мило с твоей стороны, Шеннон. Я иногда скучаю. Но всегда буду поклонницей искусства. Я люблю ходить на мюзиклы, ведь это идеальное сочетание танца, песни и театра.
Elena: Spasibo za kompliment, ochen' milo s tvoeĭ storony, SHennon. ĨA inogda skuchaĩu. No vsegda budu poklonniŝseĭ iskusstva. ĨA lĩublĩu khodit' na mĩuzikly, ved' éto ideal'noe sochetanie tanŝsa, pesni i teatra.

Шеннон: Совершенно точно! Я рада, что ты все еще любишь искусство. Спасибо за приглашение. Я всегда с удовольствием хожу с тобой на мероприятия, связанные с искусством и всегда узнаю что-то новое.
SHennon: Sovershenno tochno! ĨA rada, chto ty vse eshche lĩubish' iskusstvo. Spasibo za priglashenie. ĨA vsegda s udovol'stviem khozhu s toboĭ na meropriĩatiĩa, svĩazannye s iskusstvom i vsegda uznaĩu chto-to novoe.

GOING TO SEE A MUSICAL

Shannon: What a fantastic performance! Thank you for inviting me to the musical.

Elena: You are welcome. I'm happy you enjoyed the show. The choreography of the dancers was incredible. It reminds me of when I used to dance many years ago.

Shannon: I know! You were such a talented ballerina. Do you miss dancing?

Elena: Oh, that's very kind of you, Shannon. I do miss it sometimes. But I will always be a fan of the arts. That's why I love going to musicals because it's the perfect combination of dance, song and theater.

Shannon: Absolutely! I'm glad you are still an art fan too. Thank you for the invitation. It's always a pleasure to attend an arts event with you and learn something new.

23.   ПОЕЗДКА В ОТПУСК – POEZDKA V OTPUSK
TAKING A VACATION

Джули: Я только что купила билет в Нью-Йорк. Я так рада, что увижу этот город!
Dzhuli: I͡A tol'ko chto kupila bilet v N'i͡u-Ĭork. I͡A tak rada, chto uvizhu ėtot gorod!

Софи: Молодец! Путешествовать это очень интересно. Я люблю открывать для себя новые места и знакомиться с новыми людьми. Когда ты уезжаешь?
Sofi: Molodet͡s! Puteshestvovat' ėto ochen' interesno. I͡A li͡ubli͡u otkryvat' dli͡a sebi͡a novye mesta i znakomit'si͡a s novymi li͡ud'mi. Kogda ty uezzhaesh'?

Джули: На следующей неделе. Я взяла ночной рейс. Он был подешевле.
Dzhuli: Na sledui͡ushcheĭ nedele. I͡A vzi͡ala nochnoĭ reĭs. On byl podeshevle.

Надеюсь, я смогу спать в самолете.
Nadei͡us', i͡a smogu spat' v samolete.

Софи: Я бы поехала с тобой! Нью-Йорк - волшебное место. Тебе там будет очень интересно.
Sofi: I͡A by poekhala s toboĭ! N'i͡u-Ĭork - volshebnoe mesto. Tebe tam budet ochen' interesno.

Джули: Надеюсь. Я заеду к своему брату, он там живет. Я буду там неделю, а потом поеду на поезде в Вашингтон.
Dzhuli: Nadei͡us'. I͡A zaedu k svoemu bratu, on tam zhivet. I͡A budu tam nedeli͡u, a potom poedu na poezde v Vashington.

Софи: Отличная идея для отпуска. А я с нетерпением хочу провести неделю на пляже в мой летний отпуск. Просто хочу отдохнуть.
Sofi: Otlichnai͡a idei͡a dli͡a otpuska. A i͡a s neterpeniem khochu provesti nedeli͡u na pli͡azhe v moĭ letniĭ otpusk. Prosto khochu otdokhnut'.

TAKING A VACATION

Julie: I just bought a ticket to New York City. I'm so excited to see the city!

Sophie: Good for you! Traveling is so much fun. I love discovering new places and new people. When are you leaving?

Julie: Next week. I'm taking the red eye. It was cheaper.

Hopefully, I'll be able to sleep on the plane.

Sophie: I wish I could go with you! New York City is a magical place. You will have so much fun.

Julie: I hope so. I'm going to visit my brother who lives there. I will stay for a week and then take the train down to Washington, DC

Sophie: That sounds like a great vacation. I'm looking forward to a week at the beach for my summer vacation. I just want to relax.

24. В ЗООМАГАЗИНЕ – V ZOOMAGAZINE
AT THE PET STORE

Конни: Какой красивый кот! Как он тебе?
Konni: Kakoĭ krasivyĭ kot! Kak on tebe?

Гари: Ну, я бы, пожалуй, купил собаку. Собаки более верные животные, чем кошки. А кошки просто ленивые.
Gari: Nu, ĭa by, pozhaluĭ, kupil sobaku. Sobaki bolee vernye zhivotnye, chem koshki. A koshki prosto lenivye.

Конни: Да, но им нужно уделять столько внимания! Ты бы выгуливал ее каждый день? Убирал бы за ней?
Konni: Da, no im nuzhno udeli͡at' stol'ko vnimanii͡a! Ty by vygulival ee kazhdyĭ den'? Ubiral by za neĭ?

Гари: Хмм. Точно. Может, птичку? Или рыбок?
Gari: Xmm. Tochno. Mozhet, ptichku? Ili rybok?

Конни: Нам придется потратить много денег на клетку или на аквариум. И, если честно, я даже не знаю, как ухаживать за птицами или рыбками!
Konni: Nam prideti͡a potratit' mnogo deneg na kletku ili na akvarium. I, esli chestno, ĭa dazhe ne znai͡u, kak ukhazhivat' za pti͡sami ili rybkami!

Гари: Ну, мы, по-видимому, еще не готовы заводить животное в доме.
Gari: Nu, my, po-vidimomu, eshche ne gotovy zavodit' zhivotnoe v dome.

Конни: Ха-ха...Да, ты прав. Давай купим продуктов и поговорим о них.
Konni: Xa-kha...Da, ty prav. Davaĭ kupim produktov i pogovorim o nikh.

AT THE PET STORE

Connie: What a beautiful cat! What do you think?

Gary: I think I'd rather get a dog. Dogs are more loyal than cats. Cats are just lazy.

Connie: Yes, but they need so much attention! Would you be willing to walk it every single day? And clean up after it?

Gary: Hmm. Good point. What about a bird? Or a fish?

Connie: We'd have to invest a lot of money in a cage or a fish tank. And I honestly don't know how to take care of a bird or a fish!

Gary: Well, we're obviously not ready to get a pet yet.

Connie: Haha... Yeah, you're right. Let's get some food and talk about it.

25. ВЫРАЖАЕМ СВОЕ МНЕНИЕ – VYRAZHAEM SVOE MNENIE EXPRESSING YOUR OPINION

Джейк: Куда поехать в отпуск в этом году? Нам нужно решить в ближайшее время.
Dzheĭk: Kuda poekhat' v otpusk v étom godu? Nam nuzhno reshit' v blizhaĭshee vremi͡a.

Мелисса: Ну, я бы хотела поехать куда-нибудь где тепло.. Может, на море? Или мы могли бы арендовать домик у озера.
Melissa: Nu, i͡a by khotela poekhat' kuda-nibud' gde teplo. Mozhet, na more? Ili my mogli by arendovat' domik u ozera.

Джейк: Ты опять хочешь на море? А я зимой хочу на лыжи. Мы можем пойти на компромисс и в следующем году в апреле поехать в Скалистые горы в Колорадо? Там есть красивые горнолыжные курорты.
Dzheĭk: Ty opi͡at' khochesh' na more? A i͡a zimoĭ khochu na lyzhi. My mozhem poĭti na kompromiss i v sledui͡ushchem godu v aprele poekhat' v Skalistye gory v Kolorado? Tam est' krasivye gornolyzhnye kurorty.

Мелисса: Ух ты, мы никогда не были в Колорадо! Но я не знаю, будет ли солнечно и тепло. Сначала мне нужно немного изучить вопрос. Это поможет мне принять решение.
Melissa: Ukh ty, my nikogda ne byli v Kolorado! No i͡a ne znai͡u, budet li solnechno i teplo. Snachala mne nuzhno nemnogo izuchit' vopros. Éto pomozhet mne prini͡at' reshenie.

EXPRESSING YOUR OPINION

Jake: Where should we take a vacation this year? We need to decide soon.

Melissa: Well, I'd like to go somewhere warm. How about the beach? Or we could rent a cabin on the lake.

Jake: You want to go to the beach, again? I want to ski this winter. We can compromise and travel to the Rocky Mountains in Colorado next April? There are beautiful ski resorts there.

Melissa: Oh, we've never been to Colorado before! But I don't know if it will be sunny and warm then. I need to do some research first. That will help me make a decision.

26.   Хобби – ХОВВІ
HOBBIES

Райан: Я так счастлив, что на этой неделе закончились полугодовые экзамены.
Raĭan: *ĨA tak schastliv, chto na étoĭ nedele zakonchilis' polugodovye ékzameny.*

Тайлер: Я тоже. Я никак не дождусь поездки в горы на выходных. У меня уже запланирована небольшая классная прогулка в лесу. А еще, если погода будет хорошая, я поплыву на каноэ вниз по течению реки.
Taĭler: *ĨA tozhe. ĨA nikak ne dozhdus' poezdki v gory na vykhodnykh. U meniã uzhe zaplanirovana nebol'shaiã klassnaiã progulka v lesu. A eshche, esli pogoda budet khoroshaiã, iã poplyvu na kanoé vniz po techeniiũ reki.*

Райан: Вот это здорово! А я еду в Колорадо. Я с собой захвачу камеру, ведь осень наступит очень быстро. Листья уже начали менять цвет на все оттенки красного и оранжевого. Будет очень классно.
Raĭan: *Vot éto zdorovo! A iã edu v Kolorado. ĨA s soboĭ zakhvachu kameru, ved' osen' nastupit ochen' bystro. List'iã uzhe nachali meniãt' tsvet na vse ottenki krasnogo i oranzhevogo. Budet ochen' klassno.*

Тайлер: В следующий раз, когда будешь туда ехать, возьми меня с собой. Я слышал, что в Колорадо отличная гребля на каноэ.
Taĭler: *V sleduiũshchiĭ raz, kogda budesh' tuda ekhat', voz'mi meniã s soboĭ. ĨA slyshal, chto v Kolorado otlichnaiã grebliã na kanoé.*

HOBBIES

Ryan: I'm so happy this week of midterm exams is finished.

Tyler: Same here. I'm looking forward to relaxing in the mountains this weekend. I've planned a nice little hike in the woods. Also, if the weather is good, I'm going to go canoeing down the river.

Ryan: Oh, how fun! I'm going to Colorado. I'm taking my camera because fall is coming fast. The leaves are already turning all shades of red and orange. It will be awesome.

Tyler: Next time you go there, I'll join you. I've heard Colorado is a great place to go canoeing.

27. СВАДЬБА – SVAD''BA
THE WEDDING

Анджелика: Ну разве невеста не очаровательна в этом свадебном платье?
Andzhelika: Nu razve nevesta ne ocharovatel'na v étom svadebnom plat'e?

Мария: Выглядит шикарно. И жених такой романтичный. Мне только что рассказали историю их помолвки! Он сделал ей предложение во время ужина при свечах в Париже. Они там учились в школе.
Mariĩa: Vygliãdit shikarno. I zhenikh takoĭ romantichnyĭ. Mne tol'ko chto rasskazali istoriĩu ikh pomolvki! On sdelal eĭ predlozhenie vo vremiã uzhina pri svechakh v Parizhe. Oni tam uchilis' v shkole.

Анджелика: Да? Замечательно. А медовый месяц! Большинство после женитьбы едут на море на недельку. Мне кажется, это очень скучная идея. Вместо этого они планируют поехать в Калифорнию и проехаться по побережью на мотоцикле.
Andzhelika: Da? Zamechatel'no. A medovyĭ mesiãts! Bol'shinstvo posle zhenit'by edut na more na nedel'ku. Mne kazhetsiã, éto ochen' skuchnaiã ideiã. Vmesto étogo oni planiruiũt poekhat' v Kaliforniĩu i proekhat'siã po poberezh'iũ na mototsikle.

Мария: Правда? Шикарная идея! Кстати, пока что это самая лучшая свадьба, на которой я когда-либо была!
Mariĩa: Pravda? SHikarnaiã ideiã! Kstati, poka chto éto samaiã luchshaiã svad'ba, na kotoroĭ iã kogda-libo byla!

THE WEDDING

Angelica: Doesn't the bride look beautiful in that wedding dress?

Maria: Yes. She looks amazing. And the groom is such a romantic.

I just heard the story of how they got engaged! He proposed to her during a candlelight dinner in Prague. That was where they went to school.

Angelica: Oh yea? Wonderful. And the honeymoon! What a great idea! Most people just go to the beach for a week after they tie the knot. I think that's such a boring idea. Instead, they plan on going to California and cruising the coast on their motorcycle.

Maria: Really! What a fantastic idea. This is by far the best wedding I've ever been to in my life!

28. ДАВАТЬ СОВЕТ – DAVAT'' SOVET
GIVING ADVICE

Лейла: Спасибо, что встретилась со мной в обеденный перерыв. Спасибо.
Leĭla: Spasibo, chto vstretilas' so mnoĭ v obedennyĭ pereryv. Spasibo.

Моника: Нет проблем. Я рада тебе помочь. В чем проблема?
Monika: Net problem. ĬA rada tebe pomoch'. V chem problema?

Лейла: Ну, понимаешь, дело обычное. Я должна прнять решение в ближайшее время ... Соглашаться ли мне на эту новую работу? Или остаться на нынешней?
Leĭla: Nu, ponimaesh', delo obychnoe. ĬA dolzhna prnia͡t' reshenie v blizhaĭshee vremia͡ ... Soglashat'sia͡ li mne na étu novuiu͡ rabotu? Ili ostat'sia͡ na nyneshneĭ?

Моника: Ну, мне кажется, пора что-то менять, разве не так? Они выдают зарплату тебе поздно, ты недовольна. Причин более, чем достаточно, чтобы бросить эту работу.
Monika: Nu, mne kazhetsia͡, pora chto-to menia͡t', razve ne tak? Oni vydaiu͡t zarplatu tebe pozdno, ty nedovol'na. Prichin bolee, chem dostatochno, chtoby brosit' étu rabotu.

Лейла: Ты действительно так думаешь?
Leĭla: Ty deĭstvitel'no tak dumaesh'?

Моника: Я знаю это. И я слышу твои жалобы уже больше года. Поверь мне. Возьми новую работу. Что тебе терять?
Monika: ĬA znaiu͡ éto. I ia͡ slyshu tvoi zhaloby uzhe bol'she goda. Pover' mne. Voz'mi novuiu͡ rabotu. CHto tebe teria͡t'?

Лейла: Ладно, убедила. Ты всегда советуешь мне только лучшее.
Leĭla: Ladno, ubedila. Ty vsegda sovetuesh' mne tol'ko luchshee.

GIVING ADVICE

Layla: Thanks for meeting with me during your lunch hour. I appreciate it.

Monica: No problem. I'm happy to help. What's happening?

Layla: Oh you know, the usual. I have to decide soon... Should I take this new job? Or do I stick with my current one?

Monica: Well, I think it's time for a change, don't you? They pay you late and you are unhappy. That's more than enough reasons to quit your job.

Layla: Do you really think so?

Monica: I know so. And I've been listening to you complain for over a year now. Trust me. Take the job. What do you have to lose?

Layla: Ok, you convinced me. You have always given me the best advice.

29. Обучение детей – obucheniye DETEY
Teaching Children

Сэм: Привет, Джек, как прошел твой день?
Sėm: Privet, Dzhek, kak proshel tvoĭ denʹ?

Джек: Привет, Сэм, где ты был? Я искал тебя.
Dzhek: Privet, Sėm, gde ty byl? ĪA iskal tebīa.

Сэм: Ты не поверишь, но я так интересно провел время. Я провел целый день с кучей детей!
Sėm: Ty ne poverishʹ, no īa tak interesno provel vremīa. ĪA provel t͡selyĭ denʹ s kucheĭ deteĭ!

Джек: Интересно. Расскажи мне побольше.
Dzhek: Interesno. Rasskazhi mne pobolʹshe.

Сэм: Да, я провел время замечательно ... но это было так утомительно! Я не ожидал, что у детей столько энергии.
Sėm: Da, īa provel vremīa zamechatelʹno ... no ėto bylo tak utomitelʹno! ĪA ne ozhidal, chto u deteĭ stolʹko ėnergii.

Джек: Где ты встретился со всеми этими детьми?
Dzhek: Gde ty vstretilsīa so vsemi ėtimi detʹmi?

Сэм: В начальной школе в Чикаго. У меня была возможность посмотреть некоторые их занятия утром. После обеда у нас был урок базового английского с играми в слова.
Sėm: V nachalʹnoĭ shkole v CHikago. U menīa byla vozmozhnostʹ posmotretʹ nekotorye ikh zanīatiīa utrom. Posle obeda u nas byl urok bazovogo angliĭskogo s igrami v slova.

Джек: Скорее всего, английский, был для них очень сложным.
Dzhek: Skoree vsego, angliĭskiĭ, byl dlīa nikh ochenʹ slozhnym.

Сэм: Удивительно, но все они очень хотели учиться. Честно говоря, я был впечатлен.
Sėm: Udivitel'no, no vse oni ochen' khoteli uchit'sîa. CHestno govorîa, îa byl vpechatlen.

Джек: Отлично. Чему ты в итоге их научил?
Dzhek: Otlichno. CHemu ty v itoge ikh nauchil?

Сэм: Дети любят повторять вслух! Иногда я выкрикивал предложения, а они кричали мне в ответ. Я шептал, и они шептали мне в ответ. Это было так здорово!
Sėm: Deti lîubîat povtorîat' vslukh! Inogda îa vykrikival predlozheniîa, a oni krichali mne v otvet. ÎA sheptal, i oni sheptali mne v otvet. Ėto bylo tak zdorovo!

Джек: Слушай, когда я был студентом по обмену, у нас никогда не было таких уроков английского. Я рад, что у детей был такой замечательный опыт.
Dzhek: Slushaĭ, kogda îa byl studentom po obmenu, u nas nikogda ne bylo takikh urokov angliĭskogo. ÎA rad, chto u deteĭ byl takoĭ zamechatel'nyĭ opyt.

TEACHING CHILDREN

Sam: Hi Jack, how was your day?

Jack: Hi Sam, where have you been? I've been looking for you.

Sam: You won't believe the interesting experience I just had. I spent the whole day with a ton of children!

Jack: That sounds like fun. Tell me more.

Sam: Yes, it was a great time... but it was so exhausting! I didn't realize that kids have so much energy.

Jack: Where did you meet all these kids?

Sam: At the elementary school in Chicago. I had an opportunity to visit some of their classes in the morning. After that I taught them some basic English with word games in the afternoon.

Jack: I'm sure English was probably very difficult for them.

Sam: Surprisingly, they were all very eager to learn. Honestly, I was impressed.

Jack: That's great. What did you end up teaching them?

Sam: The kids love to repeat things out loud! Sometimes I yelled out the sentences, and they yelled back at me. I whispered, and they whispered back. It was so much fun!

Jack: You know, when I was a foreign exchange student, we never had English lessons like that. It makes me happy the children had such a wonderful experience.

30. ИГРАЕМ В ТЕННИС – IGRAEM V TENNIS
FUN WITH TENNIS

Альма: Себастьян, покажи мне, пожалуйста, как держать ракетку.
Al'ma: Sebast'i̯an, pokazhi mne, pozhaluĭsta, kak derzhat' raketku.

Себастьян: Конечно, Альма, это примерно так, когда мы пожимаем друг другу руки. Протяни руку, как будто ты собираешься пожать мне руку ...
Sebast'i̯an: Konechno, Al'ma, ėto primerno tak, kogda my pozhimaem drug drugu ruki. Proti̯ani ruku, kak budto ty sobiraesh'si̯a pozhat' mne ruku ...

Альма: Вот так?
Al'ma: Vot tak?

Себастьян: Да, вот так. Теперь возьми ракетку в руку, вот так.
Sebast'i̯an: Da, vot tak. Teper' voz'mi raketku v ruku, vot tak.

Альма: Теперь я готова бить по мячу, как профессионал!
Al'ma: Teper' i̯a gotova bit' po mi̯achu, kak professional!

Себастьян: Хаха, ну почти! Помни, что я тебе сказал. Есть только два типа удара: удар справа и слева.
Sebast'i̯an: Xakha, nu pochti! Pomni, chto i̯a tebe skazal. Est' tol'ko dva tipa udara: udar sprava i sleva.

Альма: Хорошо, я запомнила. Ты сказал, что удар правой рукой, который идет справа от меня, это как удар по мячу для пинг-понга.
Al'ma: Xorosho, i̯a zapomnila. Ty skazal, chto udar pravoĭ rukoĭ, kotoryĭ idet sprava ot meni̯a, ėto kak udar po mi̯achu dli̯a ping-ponga.

Себастьян: Все правильно. Попробуй сейчас. Готова? Бей!
Sebast'i̯an: Vse pravil'no. Poprobuĭ seĭchas. Gotova? Beĭ!

Альма: Упс! Я совсем пропустила его!
Al'ma: Ups! I͡A sovsem propustila ego!

Себастьян: Все нормально, давай еще раз.
Sebast'i͡an: Vse normal'no, davaĭ eshche raz.

Альма: О, я поняла. Дай мне попробовать еще раз...
Al'ma: O, i͡a poni͡ala. Daĭ mne poprobovat' eshche raz...

Себастьян: А вот еще мяч ... Ух ты! Ты отправила его через забор! Ты очень сильная.
Sebast'i͡an: A vot eshche mi͡ach ... Ukh ty! Ty otpravila ego cherez zabor! Ty ochen' sil'nai͡a.

Альма: Хаха. Я думаю, мне нужно больше тренироваться!
Al'ma: Xakha. I͡A dumai͡u, mne nuzhno bol'she trenirovat'si͡a!

FUN WITH TENNIS

Alma: Sebastian, could you show me how to hold the racket?

Sebastian: Sure Alma, it's just like when we shake hands. Hold your hand out as if you were about to shake my hand...

Alma: Just like this?

Sebastian: Yes, just like that. Now, put the racket in your hand, like this.

Alma: Now I'm ready to hit the ball like a professional!

Sebastian: Haha, almost! Remember what I told you. There are only two types of swings, the forehand and the backhand.

Alma: Ok, I remember. You said hitting a forehand, starting on my right, is like hitting a ping pong ball.

Sebastian: That's right. Give it a try now. Are you ready? Hit this!

Alma: Oops! I completely missed it!

Sebastian: That's alright, try again.

Alma: Oh, I see. Let me try again...

Sebastian: Here comes another ball... Wow! You hit it over the fence! You're a very powerful lady.

Alma: Haha. I guess I need to practice more!

31. Жизнь в Калифорнии – zhizn' v Kalifornii
LIVING IN CALIFORNIA

Джессика: Сегодня так холодно.
Dzhessika: *Segodnîa tak kholodno.*

Татьяна: Да, конечно. Рано утром мне пришлось опрыскивать лобовое стекло, оно было покрыто инеем.
Tat'îana: *Da, konechno. Rano utrom mne prishlos' opryskivat' lobovoe steklo, ono bylo pokryto ineem.*

Джессика: Я никогда бы не подумала, что в начале декабря может быть так холодно, особенно в Калифорнии.
Dzhessika: *ÎA nikogda by ne podumala, chto v nachale dekabrîa mozhet byt' tak kholodno, osobenno v Kalifornii.*

Татьяна: Это да. Когда я проснулась сегодня, температура была +4 по Цельсию. Как только я встала с постели, мне стало холодно. Холодная погода, конечно, не очень приятный сюрприз.
Tat'îana: *Ėto da. Kogda îa prosnulas' segodnîa, temperatura byla 4 po TSel'sîu. Kak tol'ko îa vstala s posteli, mne stalo kholodno. Xolodnaîa pogoda, konechno, ne ochen' priîatnyĭ sîurpriz.*

Джессика: Я даже и не припомню, когда было по-настоящему холодно в декабре.
Dzhessika: *ÎA dazhe i ne pripomnîu, kogda bylo po-nastoîashchemu kholodno v dekabre.*

Татьяна: Хуже всего то, что сегодня днем будет дождь. Будет холодно и сыро!
Tat'îana: *Xuzhe vsego to, chto segodnîa dnem budet dozhd'. Budet kholodno i syro!*

Джессика: Фу! Днем будет дождь?
Dzhessika: Fu! Dnem budet dozhd'?

Татьяна: Не только днем, но и всю оставшуюся неделю. В новостях передавали, что моросящий дождь начнется незадолго до 12 дня, а затем к четырем часам начнется очень сильный дождь.
Tat'i͡ana: Ne tol'ko dnem, no i vsi͡u ostavshui͡usi͡a nedeli͡u. V novosti͡akh peredavali, chto morosi͡ashchiǐ dozhd' nachnetsi͡a nezadolgo do 12 dni͡a, a zatem k chetyrem chasam nachnetsi͡a ochen' sil'nyǐ dozhd'.

Джессика: Получается, на этой неделе нет никаких признаков улучшения погоды?
Dzhessika: Poluchaetsi͡a, na étoǐ nedele net nikakikh priznakov uluchsheni͡i͡a pogody?

Татьяна: К субботе маловато солнца. Но перед солнечными днями в эти выходные будет туманно, ветрено и дождливо.
Tat'i͡ana: K subbote malovato solnt͡sa. No pered solnechnymi dni͡ami v éti vykhodnye budet tumanno, vetreno i dozhdlivo.

Джессика: Мне нравится, что идет дождь, хотя я не люблю дождливую погоду. У нас очень сухой сезон в этом году.
Dzhessika: Mne nravitsi͡a, chto idet dozhd', khoti͡a i͡a ne li͡ubli͡u dozhdlivui͡u pogodu. U nas ochen' sukhoǐ sezon v étom godu.

Татьяна: Да, я плохо помню, когда в последний раз шел дождь. Ну, пока нет грома или молнии, я могу потерпеть.
Tat'i͡ana: Da, i͡a plokho pomni͡u, kogda v posledniǐ raz shel dozhd'. Nu, poka net groma ili molnii, i͡a mogu poterpet'.

Джессика: У нас редко бывает гроза в Калифорнии.
Dzhessika: U nas redko byvaet groza v Kalifornii.

Татьяна: Нам очень повезло, что в Калифорнии одни из лучших погодных условий в Америке.
Tat'iana: Nam ochen' povezlo, chto v Kalifornii odni iz luchshikh pogodnykh usloviĭ v Amerike.

Джессика: Да, верно, есть места и похуже, где мы могли бы жить. Хорошо, урок начинается прямо сейчас, так что увидимся позже.
Dzhessika: Da, verno, est' mesta i pokhuzhe, gde my mogli by zhit'. Xorosho, urok nachinaetsi͡a pri͡amo seĭchas, tak chto uvidimsi͡a pozzhe.

Татьяна: Пока.
Tat'iana: Poka.

LIVING IN CALIFORNIA

Jessica: It is so chilly this morning.

Tatiana: It certainly is. Early this morning I had to spray my car's windshield because it was covered with frost.

Jessica: I never would have thought it could be this cold in early December, especially in California.

Tatiana: I know. The temperature was 40 degrees Fahrenheit when I woke up this morning. I was freezing as soon as I got out of bed. The cold weather was definitely not a nice surprise.

Jessica: I can't remember when it was actually this cold in December.

Tatiana: What's worse is that it's going to rain this afternoon. It's going to be cold and wet!

Jessica: Yuck! It's going to rain this afternoon?

Tatiana: Not just this afternoon, but also the entire rest of the week. The news said that it would start to drizzle just before noon, and then it would rain really hard by four o'clock.

Jessica: I'm guessing there's no sign of better weather this week?

Tatiana: There is a slim chance of sunshine by Saturday. However, it will be foggy, windy, and rainy before the sun comes out this weekend.

Jessica: I am glad that it rains even though I do not like rainy weather. We have a very dry season so far this year.

Tatiana: Yes, I can hardly remember when it rained last time. Well, as long as there is no thunder or lightning, I can stand it.

Jessica: We rarely have thunder or lightning in California.

Tatiana: We are very lucky that California has one of the best weather conditions in America.

Jessica: You are right, there are worse places we could be living. Alright, class is starting right now so I'll see you later.

Tatiana: See you later.

32. Приготовление выпечки –
PRIGOTOVLENIE VYPECHKI
BAKING

Челси: Мама, что ты готовишь? Пахнет так вкусно.
CHelsi: Mama, chto ty gotovish'? Pakhnet tak vkusno.

Миссис Келли: Я пеку. А вот твой любимый морковный кекс.
Missis Kelli: I͡A peku. A vot tvoĭ li͡ubimyĭ morkovnyĭ keks.

Челси: Выглядит просто потрясающе. И я вижу маффины там тоже. У тебя много дел, да?
CHelsi: Vygli͡adit prosto potri͡asai͡ushche. I i͡a vizhu maffiny tam tozhe. U tebi͡a mnogo del, da?

Миссис Келли: Да. Донован должен взять с собой несколько на день рождения завтра. Поэтому, эти маффины только для него. Смотри, не ешь их.
Missis Kelli: Da. Donovan dolzhen vzi͡at' s soboĭ neskol'ko na den' rozhdeni͡ia zavtra. Poėtomu, ėti maffiny tol'ko dli͡a nego. Smotri, ne esh' ikh.

Челси: Можно мне кусочек морковного кекса? Я сейчас очень хочу получить наслаждение от жизни.
CHelsi: Mozhno mne kusochek morkovnogo keksa? I͡A seĭchas ochen' khochu poluchit' naslazhdenie ot zhizni.

Миссис Келли: Ты не хочешь подождать до обеда?
Missis Kelli: Ty ne khochesh' podozhdat' do obeda?

Челси: Кекс говорит мне: «Челси, съешь меня... съешь меня...». Нет, я не хочу ждать. Можно, мама?
CHelsi: Keks govorit mne: «CHelsi, s"esh' meni͡a... s"esh' meni͡a...». Net, i͡a ne khochu zhdat'. Mozhno, mama?

Миссис Келли: Ха-ха ... Ладно, ешь.
Missis Kelli: Xa-kha ... Ladno, esh'.

Челси: Ням! А что на ужин сегодня вечером?
CHelsi: N͡iam! A chto na uzhin segodn͡ia vecherom?

Миссис Келли: Я сделаю ростбиф и грибной крем-суп.
Missis Kelli: ͡IA sdela͡iu rostbif i gribno͡ĭ krem-sup.

Челси: Давно ты не готовила грибной крем-суп. Тебе нужна помощь, мама?
CHelsi: Davno ty ne gotovila gribno͡ĭ krem-sup. Tebe nuzhna pomoshch', mama?

Миссис Келли: Нет, иди делай домашнее задание и дай я буду готовить.
Missis Kelli: Net, idi dela͡ĭ domashnee zadanie i da͡ĭ ͡ia budu gotovit'.

Челси: Спасибо, мама. Позови меня, когда ужин будет готов. Я не хочу опаздывать на ростбиф, крем-суп из грибов, морковный пирог и маффины.
CHelsi: Spasibo, mama. Pozovi men͡ia, kogda uzhin budet gotov. ͡IA ne khochu opazdyvat' na rostbif, krem-sup iz gribov, morkovny͡ĭ pirog i maffiny.

Миссис Келли: Маффины для Донована. Не трогай их!
Missis Kelli: Maffiny dl͡ia Donovana. Ne troga͡ĭ ikh!

Челси: Я знаю, мама. Я просто шучу.
CHelsi: ͡IA zna͡iu, mama. ͡IA prosto shuchu.

BAKING

Chelsea: Mom, what are you cooking? It smells so good.

Mrs. Kelly: I am baking cakes. This is your favorite carrot cake.

Chelsea: It looks scrumptious. And I see muffins some over there too. You have been busy, haven't you?

Mrs. Kelly: Yes. Donovan has to take some to a birthday party tomorrow. So, those muffins are just for him. Don't eat them.

Chelsea: Can I have a piece of carrot cake? I want to enjoy life right now.

Mrs. Kelly: You don't want to wait until after dinner?

Chelsea: The cake is calling my name, "Chelsea, eat me... eat me..." No, I don't want to wait. Can I, mom?

Mrs. Kelly: Ha ha... Ok, go ahead.

Chelsea: Yum! So what's for dinner tonight?

Mrs. Kelly: I will make roast beef and cream of mushroom soup.

Chelsea: It has been a long time since you made cream of mushroom soup. Do you need any help, mom?

Mrs. Kelly: No, go do your homework and leave the cooking to me.

Chelsea: Thanks, mom. Call me whenever dinner is ready. I do not want to be late for roast beef, cream of mushroom soup, carrot cake and muffins.

Mrs. Kelly: The muffins are for Donovan. Do not touch them!

Chelsea: I know, mom. I'm just kidding.

33. ПОМОЩЬ ПО ТЕЛЕФОНУ – POMOSHCH'' PO TELEFONU
HELP OVER THE PHONE

Джиджи: Спасибо за ваш звонок в Центр спорта и отдыха. Чем могу вам помочь?
Dzhidzhi: Spasibo za vash zvonok v T͡Sentr sporta i otdykha. CHem mogu vam pomoch'?

Колетт: Я купила велотренажер в вашем магазине пару месяцев назад, и у меня с ним возникли проблемы. Он перестал работать, и мне нужно отремонтировать его.
Kolett: I͡A kupila velotrenazher v vashem magazine paru mesi͡at͡sev nazad, i u meni͡a s nim voznikli problemy. On perestal rabotat', i mne nuzhno otremontirovat' ego.

Джиджи: Я соединю вас с сервисным отделом. Секундочку, пожалуйста.
Dzhidzhi: I͡A soedini͡u vas s servisnym otdelom. Sekundochku, pozhalui͡sta.

Анджела: Сервисный отдел, это Анджела. Чем могу вам помочь?
Andzhela: Servisnyĭ otdel, ėto Anzhela. CHem mogu vam pomoch'?

Колетт: В прошлом году я купила велотренажер в Центре Спорта, и его нужно починить.
Kolett: V proshlom godu i͡a kupila velotrenazher v T͡Sentre Sporta, i ego nuzhno pochinit'.

Анджела: В чем проблема?
Andzhela: V chem problema?

Колетт: Я не знаю, что случилось, но экран компьютера черный и больше не включается.
Kolett: I͡A ne znai͡u, chto sluchilos', no ėkran komp'i͡utera chernyĭ i bol'she ne vkli͡uchaetsi͡a.

Анджела: Вы пытались нажать кнопку «Пуск»?
Andzhela: Vy pytalis' nazhat' knopku «Pusk»?

Колетт: Да, и ничего не происходит.
Kolett: Da, i nichego ne proiskhodit.

Анджела: Какая у вас модель тренажера?
Andzhela: Kakaia u vas model' trenazhera?

Колетт: Skull Crusher 420Z +, с очень классной корзиной спереди.
Kolett: Skull Crusher 420Z , s ochen' klassnoĭ korzinoĭ speredi.

Анджела: Я могу отправить мастера, чтоб посмотрел ваш тренажер. Работа будет стоить 5000 долларов. Кроме того, если мы должны заменить какие-либо детали, это будет дополнительная цена. Хорошее предложение?
Andzhela: ÎA mogu otpravit' mastera, chtob posmotrel vash trenazher. Rabota budet stoit' 5000 dollarov. Krome togo, esli my dolzhny zamenit' kakie-libo detali, éto budet dopolnitel'naîa tsena. Xoroshee predlozhenie?

Колетт: Это дорого. Не покрывается ли стоимость ремонта гарантийной страховкой?
Kolett: Éto dorogo. Ne pokryvaetsîa li stoimost' remonta garantiĭnoĭ strakhovkoĭ?

Анджела: Когда вы купили велосипед?
Andzhela: Kogda vy kupili velosiped?

Колетт: около 3 месяцев назад.
Kolett: okolo 3 mesîatsev nazad.

Анджела: Простите. Стандартная гарантия распространяется только на 1 месяц. Вы купили дополнительную гарантийную страховку во время покупки?
Andzhela: Prostite. Standartnaĭa garantiĭa rasprostraniаetsĭa tol'ko na 1 mesĭat͡s. Vy kupili dopolnitel'nuĭu garantiĭnuĭu strakhovku vo vremĭa pokupki?

Колетт: Нет, я не покупала. Есть ли другие варианты, кроме оплаты 5000 долларов США за ремонт?
Kolett: Net, ĭa ne pokupala. Est' li drugie varianty, krome oplaty 5000 dollarov SSHA za remont?

Анджела: Боюсь, что нет.
Andzhela: Boĭus', chto net.

Колетт: Черт.
Kolett: CHert.

HELP OVER THE PHONE

Gigi: Thank you for calling Sports Recreation Center. How may I help you?

Colette: I purchased an exercise bike from your store a couple months ago, and I am having problems with it. It stopped working and I need to have it repaired.

Gigi: Let me connect you to the Service department. One moment please.

Angela: Service department, this is Angela. How can I help you?

Colette: I bought an exercise bike from Sports Center last year and it needs to be repaired.

Angela: What seems to be the problem?

Colette: I am not sure what happened, but the computer screen is black and doesn't turn on anymore.

Angela: Did you try to press the Start button?

Colette: Yes, and nothing turns on.

Angela: What is your bike model?

Colette: It is a Skull Crusher 420Z+, it's the one with the really cool basket in the front.

Angela: I can send a technician out to take a look at your bike. It will cost $5,000.00 for labor. Also, if we have to replace any parts, that will be extra. Sound like a deal?

Colette: That is expensive. Isn't the repair cost covered by warranty?

Angela: When did you purchase your bike?

Colette: About 3 months ago.

Angela: I am sorry. The standard warranty only covers 1 month. Did you buy extra warranty coverage at the time of purchase?

Colette: No, I did not. Are there any other options besides paying $5,000.00 for repair labor?

Angela: No, I am afraid not.

Colette: Dang it.

34.   ПОЙДЕМ НА КОНЦЕРТ – POĬDEM NA KONTSERT
LET'S GO TO A CONCERT

Кит: Слушайте, Даниэль, Саймон, сегодня вечером в парке будет концерт с отличным составом. Хотите пойти?
Kit: Slushaĭte, Daniėl', Saĭmon, segodnîa vecherom v parke budet kontsert s otlichnym sostavom. Xotite poĭti?

Даниэль: Я не работаю вечером, поэтому я точно могу.
Daniėl': ÎA ne rabotaîu vecherom, poėtomi îa tochno mogu.

Саймон: Я тоже, пойдемте!
Saĭmon: ÎA tozhe, poĭdemte!

Даниэль: Сегодня вечером очень много трафика...
Daniėl': Segodnîa vecherom ochen' mnogo trafika...

Саймон: Да, почему так много машин?
Saĭmon: Da, pochemu tak mnogo mashin?

Кит: Люди, наверное, едут все в парк на концерт. Это очень популярная группа, и у них очень классная музыка.
Kit: Lîudi, navernoe, edut vse v park na kontsert. Ėto ochen' populîarnaîa gruppa, i u nikh ochen' klassnaîa muzyka.

Даниэль: Да, играют отлично. За последние четыре года я ни разу не пропустил ни одного концерта. Каждый раз, когда я узнаю, что группа приезжает в город, я сразу покупаю билет.
Daniėl': Da, igraîut otlichno. Za poslednie chetyre goda îa ni razu ne propustil ni odnogo kontserta. Kazhdyĭ raz, kogda îa uznaîu, chto gruppa priezzhaet v gorod, îa srazu pokupaîu bilet.

Саймон: Как давно они стали играть здесь у нас?
Saĭmon: Kak davno oni stali igrat' zdes' u nas?

Даниэль: Они начали традицию шесть лет назад, и теперь каждый год они играют всю первую неделю июня.
Daniėl': Oni nachali traditsiĩu shest' let nazad, i teper' kazhdyĭ god oni igraĩut vsĩu pervuĩu nedelĩu iĩuniĩa.

Кит: Саймон, тебе действительно понравится этот вечер. Там будет отличная музыка, многие будут прыгать и громко кричать. У них даже может быть танцевальная площадка перед сценой.
Kit: Saĭmon, tebe deĭstvitel'no ponravitsĩa étot vecher. Tam budet otlichnaĩa muzyka, mnogie budut prygat' i gromko krichat'. U nikh dazhe mozhet byt' tantɕeval'naĩa ploshchadka pered stɕenoĭ.

Саймон: Не могу дождаться уже, будет очень весело.
Saĭmon: Ne mogu dozhdat'sĩa uzhe, budet ochen' veselo.

Даниэль: Я люблю гангстерский рэп. Но, должен сказать, что музыку кантри тоже приятно слушать Удивительно, но я могу слушать это целый день.
Daniėl': ĨA lĩublĩu gangsterskiĭ rėp. No, dolzhen skazat', chto muzyku kantri tozhe priĩatno slushat' Udivitel'no, no ĩa mogu slushat' éto tɕselyĭ den'.

Кит: Саймон, какую музыку ты любишь?
Kit: Saĭmon, kakuĩu muzyku ty lĩubish'?

Саймон: О, я люблю любой жанр музыки, если только она не агрессивная.
Saĭmon: O, ĩa lĩublĩu lĩuboĭ zhanr muzyki, esli tol'ko ona ne agressivnaĩa.

Даниэль: Ничего себе, стадион забит людьми! Меня удивляет количество людей, которые уже пришли на концерт. Хорошо, что мы уже здесь!
Daniėl': Nichego sebe, stadion zabit lĩud'mi! Menĩa udivlĩaet kolichestvo lĩudeĭ, kotorye uzhe prishli na kontɕsert. Xorosho, chto my uzhe zdes'!

LET'S GO TO A CONCERT

Keith: Hey Danielle, Simon, there is a concert in the park tonight with a great line up. Do you want to go?

Danielle: I don't work tonight so I can definitely go.

Simon: Me too, let's go!

Danielle: There's a ton of cars out tonight...

Simon: Yea, why is the traffic so heavy?

Keith: People are probably heading toward the park for the concert. It's a very popular band and they play really good music.

Danielle: Yes, they do. For the last four years, I have never missed one of their concerts. Every time I find out that the band is coming to town I buy a ticket right away.

Simon: How long ago did the band start playing here locally?

Danielle: They started a tradition six years ago and now every year they play the whole first week of June.

Keith: Simon, you are really going to enjoy this evening. There will be good great music, a lot of jumping around, and definitely a lot of shouting. They may even have a mosh pit.

Simon: I can't wait, it sounds like a lot fun.

Danielle: My favorite is gangster rap music; however, I have to say that country music can be pleasant to listen to. Surprisingly, I can listen to it all day long.

Keith: Simon, what kind of music do you like?

Simon: Oh, I like all kinds of music as long as it is not aggressive.

Danielle: Wow, the stadium is packed with people! I'm surprised at the number of people who have already shown up for the concert. It's a good thing we're here already!

35. Составляем план – SOSTAVLĪAEM PLAN
MAKING PLANS

Конни: Лиза, скажи мне ... Какие у тебя планы на эти выходные?
Konni: Liza, skazhi mne ... Kakie u tebīa plany na éti vykhodnye?

Лиза: Я не знаю. Ты хочешь собраться и сделать что-нибудь?
Liza: ĪA ne znaīu. Ty khochesh' sobrat'sīa i sdelat' chto-nibud'?

Сара: Как тебе кино? В AMC 24 на Паркер-роуд сейчас идет *Если ты меня покинешь, я тебя удалю.*
Sara: Kak tebe kino? V AMC 24 na Parker-roud seĭchas idet Esli ty menīa pokinesh', īa tebīa udalīu.

Конни: Я давно хотела его посмотреть! Ты читаешь мои мысли. Хотите пойти поужинать перед фильмом?
Konni: ĪA davno khotela ego posmotret'! Ty chitaesh' moi mysli. Xotite poĭti pouzhinat' pered fil'mom?

Сара: Я не хочу. Где ты хочешь встретиться?
Sara: ĪA ne khochu. Gde ty khochesh' vstretit'sīa?

Лиза: Давайте встретимся в Ред Рустер Хаус. Я давно там не была.
Liza: Davaĭte vstretimsīa v Red Ruster Xaus. ĪA davno tam ne byla.

Конни: Опять хорошая идея. Я слышала, они начали подавать новую пасту. Должно быть классно, ведь в Ред Рустер Хаус всегда была лучшая итальянская еда в городе.
Konni: Opīat' khoroshaīa ideīa. ĪA slyshala, oni nachali podavat' novuīu pastu. Dolzhno byt' klassno, ved' v Red Ruster Xaus vsegda byla luchshaīa ital'īanskaīa eda v gorode.

Сара: Когда встречаемся?
Sara: Kogda vstrechaemsīa?

95

Лиза: Ну, фильм идет в 13:00, 14:00, 16:00 и 18:00.
Liza: Nu, fil'm idet v 13:00, 14:00, 16:00 i 18:00.

Конни: Почему бы нам не пойти на 16:00? Мы можем встретиться в Ред Рустер Хаус в 13:00. И у нас будет достаточно времени.
Konni: Pochemu by nam ne poĭti na 16:00? My mozhem vstretit'si͡a v Red Ruster Xaus v 13:00. I u nas budet dostatochno vremeni.

MAKING PLANS

Connie: Lisa, tell me... What are your plans for this upcoming weekend?

Lisa: I don't know. Do you want to get together and do something?

Sarah: How do you feel about going to see a movie? AMC 24 on Parker Road is showing *If You Leave Me, I Delete You.*

Connie: I've been wanting to see that! It's like you read my mind. Do you want to go out to dinner beforehand?

Sarah: That's fine with me. Where do you want to meet?

Lisa: Let's meet at the Red Rooster House. It's been a while since I've been there.

Connie: Good idea again. I heard they just came out with a new pasta. It should be good because Red Rooster House always has the best Italian food in town.

Sarah: When should we meet?

Lisa: Well, the movie is showing at 1:00PM, 2:00PM, 4:00PM and 6:00PM.

Connie: Why don't we go to the 4:00PM show? We can meet at Red Rooster House at 1PM. That will give us enough time.

36. Зимние каникулы – ZIMNIE KANIKULY
WINTER BREAK

Трент: Привет, Джаред, если ты готов ехать, бросай все свои вещи в багажник и садись на переднее сиденье.
Trent: Privet, Dzhared, esli ty gotov ekhat', brosaĭ vse svoi veshchi v bagazhnik i sadis' na perednee siden'e.

Джаред: Хорошо, Трент. Спасибо, что подвез меня до дома. Обычно мои родители забирают меня, но они сегодня работают допоздна.
Dzhared: Xorosho, Trent. Spasibo, chto podvez meni͡a do doma. Obychno moi roditeli zabirai͡ut meni͡a, no oni segodni͡a rabotai͡ut dopozdna.

Трент: Не переживай, я рад, что смог помочь.
Trent: Ne perezhivaĭ, i͡a rad, chto smog pomoch'.

Джаред: Кстати, когда следующий баскетбольный матч?
Dzhared: Kstati, kogda sledui͡ushchiĭ basketbol'nyĭ match?

Трент: Где-то после зимних каникул уже, но в любом случае далеко еще. У тебя есть планы на каникулы?
Trent: Gde-to posle zimnikh kanikul uzhe, no v li͡ubom sluchae daleko eshche. U tebi͡a est' plany na kanikuly?

Джаред: Не совсем. Кроме занятий баскетболом, я просто буду работать.
Dzhared: Ne sovsem. Krome zani͡atiĭ basketbolom, i͡a prosto budu rabotat'.

Трент: Работать? Ты получил новую работу или все еще работаешь в Twisters?
Trent: Rabotat'? Ty poluchil novui͡u rabotu ili vse eshche rabotaesh' v Twisters?

Джаред: Ну, Twisters была моей первой работой, и с людьми было здорово работать. Но график был очень сложным, это мешало ходить в школу и работать.
Dzhared: Nu, Twisters byla moeĭ pervoĭ rabotoĭ, i s li͡ud'mi bylo zdorovo rabotat'. No grafik byl ochen' slozhnym, ėto meshalo khodit' v shkolu i rabotat'.

Трент: Ну, что ты сейчас делаешь на своей новой работе?
Trent: Nu, chto ty seĭchas delaesh' na svoeĭ novoĭ rabote?

Джаред: Я работаю в сфере продаж технологий. Это в колл-центр. Сначала это было немного сложно, но теперь я привык разговаривать по телефону с незнакомыми людьми.
Dzhared: I͡A rabotai͡u v sfere prodazh tekhnologiĭ. Ėto v koll-t͡sentr. Snachala ėto bylo nemnogo slozhno, no teper' i͡a privyk razgovarivat' po telefonu s neznakomymi li͡ud'mi.

Трент: Круто. Когда ты начал новую работу?
Trent: Kruto. Kogda ty nachal novui͡u rabotu?

Джаред: Я работаю в Techmerica с 1 октября. А у тебя какие планы на каникулы?
Dzhared: I͡A rabotai͡u v Techmerica s 1 okti͡abri͡a. A u tebi͡a kakie plany na kanikuly?

Трент: Я планирую катание на сноуборде в Аспене. Ты должен приехать, если не сильно будешь занят на новой работе.
Trent: I͡A planirui͡u katanie na snouborde v Aspene. Ty dolzhen priekhat', esli ne sil'no budesh' zani͡at na novoĭ rabote.

Джаред: Здорово! Спасибо за приглашение.
Dzhared: Zdorovo! Spasibo za priglashenie.

WINTER BREAK

Trent: Hey Jared, if you're ready to go just throw your all of your stuff in the trunk and ride in the front seat.

Jared: Alright, Trent. Thank you for giving me a ride home. Usually my parents pick me up, but they had to work late tonight.

Trent: No worries, I'm glad I could help.

Jared: By the way, when is our next basketball game?

Trent: It is sometime after winter break, but anyways it's a long time from now. Have you made any plans for the break though?

Jared: Not really. Other than going to basketball practice, I'll just be working.

Trent: Working? Did you get a new job or are you still working at Twisters?

Jared: Well, Twisters was a good first job and the people were really great to work with. However, the schedule was very demanding which made it difficult to go to school and work.

Trent: Well, what are you doing now at your new job?

Jared: I am working in technology sales. It's at a call center. It was a little difficult at first, but now I am used to talking to strangers on the phone.

Trent: Oh, that sounds great. When did you start the new job?

Jared: I have been with Techmerica since October 1st. Do you have any plans for break?

Trent: I am planning a snowboarding trip to Aspen. You should come if you're not too busy at the new job.

Jared: Oh, that sounds like fun! Thank you for the invitation.

37. Визит к врачу – VIZIT K VRACHU
VISITING THE DOCTOR

Доктор: Доброе утро, Эми.
Doktor: Dobroe utro, Ėmi.

Эми: Доброе утро, доктор.
Ėmi: Dobroe utro, doktor.

Доктор: Глядя на информацию, я вижу, что вы начали чувствовать усталость около месяца назад, а затем у вас начались мигрени. У вас было расстройство желудка и высокая температура?
Doktor: Gli͡adi͡a na informat͡sii͡u, i͡a vizhu, chto vy nachali chuvstvovat' ustalost' okolo mesi͡at͡sa nazad, a zatem u vas nachalis' migreni. U vas bylo rasstroĭstvo zheludka i vysokai͡a temperatura?

Эми: Нет, доктор.
Ėmi: Net, doktor.

Доктор: Дайте я быстро вас осмотрю. Сделайте глубокий вдох, задержите дыхание, а затем выдохните. Еще раз, пожалуйста. Вы когда-нибудь вносили какие-либо изменения в свой рацион, наблюдая колебания веса?
Doktor: Daĭte i͡a bystro vas osmotri͡u. Sdelaĭte glubokiĭ vdokh, zaderzhite dykhanie, a zatem vydokhnite. Eshche raz, pozhaluĭsta. Vy kogda-nibud' vnosili kakie-libo izmeneni͡ia v svoĭ rat͡sion, nabli͡udai͡a kolebani͡ia vesa?

Эми: Я недавно сбросила 2 кг 200 граммов, но я совсем не меняла свою диету.
Ėmi: I͡A nedavno sbrosila 2 kg 200 grammov, no i͡a sovsem ne meni͡ala svoi͡u dietu.

Доктор: Вы случайно не страдаете бессонницей?
Doktor: Vy sluchaĭno ne stradaete bessonnit͡seĭ?

Эми: Мне трудно заснуть. И я часто просыпаюсь ночью.
Émi: Mne trudno zasnut'. I i͡a chasto prosypai͡us' noch'i͡u.

Доктор: Вы пьете, курите?
Doktor: Vy p'ete, kurite?

Эми: Нет.
Émi: Net.

Доктор: Похоже на то, что у вас воспаление легких. Кроме того, я не вижу никаких других проблем. А пока вам нужно отдохнуть и делать упражнения.
Doktor: Pokhozhe na to, chto u vas vospalenie legkikh. Krome togo, i͡a ne vizhu nikakikh drugikh problem. A poka vam nuzhno otdokhnut' i delat' uprazhneni͡ia.

Я дам вам рецепт на лекарства от пневмонии. У Вас есть аллергия на какие-либо лекарства?
I͡A dam vam ret͡sept na lekarstva ot pnevmonii. U Vas est' allergii͡a na kakie-libo lekarstva?

Эми: Даже не знаю.
Émi: Dazhe ne znai͡u.

Доктор: Хорошо. Принимайте это лекарство три раза в день после еды.
Doktor: Xorosho. Prinimai̯te éto lekarstvo tri raza v den' posle edy.

Эми: Спасибо, доктор.
Émi: Spasibo, doktor.

Доктор: Пожалуйста.
Doktor: Pozhalui̯sta.

VISITING THE DOCTOR

Doctor: Good morning, Amy.

Amy: Good morning, Doctor.

Doctor: Looking at your information, I see that you started feeling tired about a month ago, and then you started having migraines.

You have also had an upset stomach and fever also?

Amy: No, doctor.

Doctor: Let me do a quick physical checkup. Please take a deep breath, hold your breath, and then exhale. One more time please. Have you made any changes to your diet seen fluctuation in your weight recently?

Amy: I lost five pounds recently, but I haven't changed my diet at all.

Doctor: By chance do you suffer from insomnia?

Amy: It is difficult for me to fall asleep when I go to bed. I also wake up a lot during the night.

Doctor: Do you drink or smoke cigarettes?

Amy: No.

Doctor: It appears that you have pneumonia. Besides that, I do not see any other problems. For now, get some rest and do some exercise.

I am going to give you a prescription for the pneumonia. Are you allergic to any medications?

Amy: Not that I am aware of.

Doctor: Alright. Take this medication three times a day after you eat.

Amy: Thank you, Doctor.

Doctor: You are welcome.

38.   РЫНОК – RYNOK
THE MARKET

Лора: Джой, перед уходом на работу утром, мама попросила меня сходить в магазин за продуктами. Проблема в том, что мне нужно закончить школьный проект. Ты можешь пойти за меня?
Lora: Dzhoĭ, pered ukhodom na rabotu utrom, mama poprosila meni͡a skhodit' v magazin za produktami. Problema v tom, chto mne nuzhno zakonchit' shkol'nyĭ proekt. Ty mozhesh' poĭti za meni͡a?

Джой: Я закончила работу по дому, поэтому могу сходить за тебя. Что мама сказала купить?
Dzhoĭ: I͡A zakonchila rabotu po domu, poétomu mogu skhodit' za tebi͡a. CHto mama skazala kupit'?

Лора: Кроме курицы, рыбы и овощей, мы можем купить все, что захотим, на закуску и завтрак. Она в основном хотела, чтобы я купила достаточно продуктов на всю неделю.
Lora: Krome kurit͡sy, ryby i ovoshcheĭ, my mozhem kupit' vse, chto zakhotim, na zakusku i zavtrak. Ona v osnovnom khotela, chtoby i͡a kupila dostatochno produktov na vsi͡u nedeli͡u.

Джой: Ты хочешь что-нибудь конкретное на завтрак?
Dzhoĭ: Ty khochesh' chto-nibud' konkretnoe na zavtrak?

Лора: Наверное, как обычно, овсянку.
Lora: Navernoe, kak obychno, ovsi͡anku.

Джой: Я не хочу овсянку каждый день. Тогда я куплю блины и сироп.
Dzhoĭ: I͡A ne khochu ovsi͡anku kazhdyĭ den'. Togda i͡a kupli͡u bliny i sirop.

Лора: Если сможешь найти, пожалуйста, купи новые безглютеновые блины в отделе здоровой еды. Мне интересно, какие они на вкус.
Lora: Esli smozhesh' naĭti, pozhaluĭsta, kupi novye bezglĭutenovye bliny v otdele zdorovoĭ edy. Mne interesno, kakie oni na vkus.

Джой: Думаешь, хватит ли еще кофе и сливок для мамы и папы?
Dzhoĭ: Dumaesh', khvatit li eshche kofe i slivok dlĭa mamy i papy?

Лора: Да. Вообще, надо купить немного молока. Закончилось.
Lora: Da. Voobshche, nado kupit' nemnogo moloka. Zakonchilos'.

Джой: Какие снэки ты хочешь?
Dzhoĭ: Kakie snėki ty khochesh'?

Лора: Я бы взяла чипсы. Ты, наверное, хочешь свои шоколадные печенья.
Lora: ĬA by vzĭala chipsy. Ty, navernoe, khochesh' svoi shokoladnye pechen'ĭa.

Джой: Зная себя, наверное, лучше записать все это, иначе я забуду их пока доберусь до рынка. Я бы не хотела ездить два раза!
Dzhoĭ: Znaĭa sebĭa, navernoe, luchshe zapisat' vse ėto, inache ĭa zabudu ikh poka doberus' do rynka. ĬA by ne khotela ezdit' dva raza!

THE MARKET

Laura: Joy, before mom left for work this morning, she asked me to go grocery shopping. The problem is that I need to finish my school project. Can you go for me?

Joy: I am finished with my chores, so I can go to the store for you. What did mom want you to buy?

Laura: Besides chicken, fish and vegetables, we can buy whatever else we want for snacks and breakfast. She basically wanted me to buy enough groceries for the entire week.

Joy: Is there anything specifically you want for breakfast?

Laura: I guess some oatmeal as usual.

Joy: I don't want oatmeal every day. I will buy some pancakes and syrup then.

Laura: If you can find it, get the new gluten free pancakes in the health section please. I want to see if it tastes any different.

Joy: Is there still enough coffee and cream for mom and dad?

Laura: Yes, we do. In fact, you should buy some milk also. We almost out of it.

Joy: Next, what do you want for snacks?

Laura: Some chips would be fine with me. You probably want your chocolate cookies.

Joy: Knowing myself it's probably better that I write all these things down or else I will forget them by the time I get to the market. I would hate to have to make two trips!

39. Давай арендуем жилье – Davaĭ arenduem zhil'e
Let's Get An Apartment

Патрик: Привет, Джош. Что ты здесь делаешь?
Patrik: Privet, Dzhosh. CHto ty zdes' delaesh'?

Джош: Я ищу квартиру в аренду. Что ты здесь делаешь? Тоже ищешь квартиру?
Dzhosh: ÎA ishchu kvartiru v arendu. CHto ty zdes' delaesh'? Tozhe ishchesh' kvartiru?

Патрик: Да. Мои родители живут далековато, поэтому я хотел бы найти квартиру ближе к школе и моей работе.
Patrik: Da. Moi roditeli zhivut dalekovato, poétomu ÎA khotel by naĭti kvartiru blizhe k shkole i moeĭ rabote.

Джош: Ну да, логично. Я до сих пор не решил, хочу ли я остаться в общежитии или жить в своей собственной квартире.
Dzhosh: Nu da, logichno. ÎA do sikh por ne reshil, khochu li ÎA ostat'sÎA v obshchezhitii ili zhit' v svoeĭ sobstvennoĭ kvartire.

Патрик: А ты что ищешь?
Patrik: A ty chto ishchesh'?

Джош: Если честно, мне много не надо. Все, что мне нужно, это достаточно места для кровати и письменного стола. Конечно, нужна кухня, чтобы можно было готовить еду и экономить немного денег.
Dzhosh: Esli chestno, mne mnogo ne nado. Vse, chto mne nuzhno, éto dostatochno mesta dlÎA krovati i pis'mennogo stola. Konechno, nuzhna kukhnÎA, chtoby mozhno bylo gotovit' edu i ékonomit' nemnogo deneg.

Патрик: Это похоже на то, что я тоже ищу. Я не могу работать полный рабочий день, как летом. Я буду учиться большую часть своего времени, поэтому я не смогу работать так много. Все, что мне нужно, это что-то безопасное, тихое и чистое.
Patrik: Éto pokhozhe na to, chto i͡a tozhe ishchu. I͡A ne mogu rabotat' polnyĭ rabochiĭ den', kak letom. I͡A budu uchit'si͡a bol'shui͡u chast' svoego vremeni, poétomu i͡a ne smogu rabotat' tak mnogo. Vse, chto mne nuzhno, éto chto-to bezopasnoe, tikhoe i chistoe.

Джош: Другая проблема – самому платить за всю квартиру. Большинство мест, которые я видел, очень дорогие.
Dzhosh: Drugai͡a problema – samomu platit' za vsi͡u kvartiru. Bol'shinstvo mest, kotorye i͡a videl, ochen' dorogie.

Патрик: А ты задумывался о проживании с кем-то? Если хочешь, мы можем найти трехкомнатную квартиру и жить там вместе. Так может быть дешевле.
Patrik: A ty zadumyvalsi͡a o prozhivanii s kem-to? Esli khochesh', my mozhem naĭti trekhkomnatnui͡u kvartiru i zhit' tam vmeste. Tak mozhet byt' deshevle.

Джош: Это может решить нашу проблему. Хочешь попробовать?
Dzhosh: Éto mozhet reshit' nashu problemu. Xochesh' poprobovat'?

Патрик: Да, возможно, это отличная идея. Давай попробуем этот вариант и посмотрим, понравится ли нам это.
Patrik: Da, vozmozhno, éto otlichnai͡a idei͡a. Davaĭ poprobuem étot variant i posmotrim, ponravitsi͡a li nam éto.

LET'S GET AN APARTMENT

Patrick: Hey, Josh. What are you doing here?

Josh: I am looking for an apartment to rent. What are you doing here? Are you looking for an apartment also?

Patrick: Yes. My parents' house is really far away so I'd like to find an apartment that is closer to school and my job.

Josh: Ok, that makes sense. I still haven't decided if I want to stay in the dorms or get my own apartment.

Patrick: So, what are you looking for?

Josh: I don't need much to be honest. All I need is a place big enough for my bed and desk. Of course, it needs to have a kitchen so that I can cook my meals and save a little bit of money.

Patrick: That sounds like what I'm looking for too. I can't work full-time like I did during the summer. I will be spending most of my time studying so I won't be able to work as much. All I need is something safe, quiet and clean.

Josh: The other issue is paying for an entire apartment for myself. Most places I have seen are very expensive.

Patrick: Have you thought about sharing an apartment? If you want, we can find a two-bedroom apartment and share it. It may be cheaper that way.

Josh: That could solve our problem. Do you want to try it?

Patrick: Yes, that could be a great idea. Let's go check this one out and see if we like it.

40. ТОРГОВЫЙ КИОСК – TORGOVYĬ KIOSK
THE CONCESSION STAND

Саймон: Там есть киоск с едой. Вы оба хотите что-нибудь?
Saĭmon: Tam est' kiosk s edoĭ. Vy oba khotite chto-nibud'?

Даниэль: Мне ничего не хочется, спасибо. У меня уже есть бутылка воды.
Daniėl': Mne nichego ne khochetsi͡a, spasibo. U meni͡a uzhe est' butylka vody.

Кит: Я хочу пакетик чипсов и холодного пива. Ты уверен, что не хочешь хот-дог, Даниэль?
Kit: I͡A khochu paketik chipsov i kholodnogo piva. Ty uveren, chto ne khochesh' khot-dog, Daniėl'?

Даниэль: Я совершенно уверен. Моя мама готовит вкусный стейк на ужин, не хочу слишком наедаться тут.
Daniėl': I͡A sovershenno uveren. Moi͡a mama gotovit vkusnyĭ steĭk na uzhin, ne khochu slishkom naedat'si͡a tut.

Кит: Даниэль, тебе так повезло, что у тебя такой хороший повар как мама. Саймон, ты должен попробовать ее черничный пирог. Честно говоря, лучшего пирога нет во всем городе.
Kit: Daniėl', tebe tak povezlo, chto u tebi͡a takoĭ khoroshiĭ povar kak mama. Saĭmon, ty dolzhen poprobovat' ee chernichnyĭ pirog. CHestno govori͡a, luchshego piroga net vo vsem gorode.

Даниэль: На самом деле, моя мама сегодня будет печь черничный пирог! Если хочешь, я оставлю тебе кусочек, Саймон.
Daniėl': Na samom dele, moi͡a mama segodni͡a budet pech' chernichnyĭ pirog! Esli khochesh', i͡a ostavli͡u tebe kusochek, Saĭmon.

Саймон: Не дразни меня! Я бы с удовольствием.
Saïmon: Ne drazni meniâ! Iâ by s udovol'stviem.

Даниэль: А тебе, Кит? Тебе тоже оставить кусок пирога?
Daniél': A tebe, Kit? Tebe tozhe ostavit' kusok piroga?

Саймон: Кит, пора купить снэки и пиво, если ты все еще хочешь. Уже почти 3 часа дня, и представление уже должно начаться.
Saïmon: Kit, pora kupit' snéki i pivo, esli ty vse eshche khochesh'. Uzhe pochti 3 chasa dniâ, i predstavlenie uzhe dolzhno nachat'siâ.

Кит: Последний шанс что-то купить. Вы уверены, что ничего не хотите?
Kit: Posledniĭ shans chto-to kupit'. Vy uvereny, chto nichego ne khotite?

Даниэль: Я уверен, спасибо Кит.
Daniél': Iâ uveren, spasibo Kit.

Саймон: Я тоже, Кит.
Saïmon: Iâ tozhe, Kit.

Кит: Хорошо, держи мое место, я сейчас вернусь.
Kit: Xorosho, derzhi moe mesto, iâ seĭchas vernus'.

THE CONCESSSION STAND

Simon: There is a food stand over there. Do you two want anything?

Danielle: Nothing for me, thanks. I already have my bottle of water.

Keith: I want a bag of chips and a cold beer. Are you sure you do not want a hot dog, Danielle?

Danielle: I am quite sure. My mom is cooking a good steak dinner, and I want to make sure I don't eat too much here.

Keith: Danielle, you are so lucky to have such a good cook for a mother. Simon, you have to taste her blueberry pie one of these days. Honestly, there's no better pie in this whole town.

Danielle: In fact, my mom is baking her blueberry pie tonight! I you would like, I will save you a piece, Simon.

Simon: Don't tease me with a good time! I would love that.

Danielle: How about you, Keith? A piece of cake for you too?

Simon: Keith, you better get your snacks and beer now if you still want them. It is almost 3:00PM, and the show is about to start.

Keith: Last chance to get something. Are you guys sure you don't want anything?

Danielle: I am sure, thank you Keith.

Simon: Me neither, Keith.

Keith: Ok, save my seat and I will be right back.

41. Время обеда – vremi͡a obeda
LUNCHTIME

Эмили: Триша, попросить твой телефон, чтобы позвонить маме после обеда?
Ėmili: *Trisha, poprosit' tvoĭ telefon, chtoby pozvonit' mame posle obeda?*

Триша: Да, конечно, Эмили. Не забудь передать ей привет.
Trisha: *Da, konechno, Ėmili. Ne zabud' peredat' eĭ privet.*

Майра: Эмили, передай перец, пожалуйста?
Maĭra: *Ėmili, peredaĭ perets, pozhaluĭsta?*

Эмили: Конечно, вот.
Ėmili: *Konechno, vot.*

Майра: И соль тоже, пожалуйста. Спасибо.
Maĭra: *I sol' tozhe, pozhaluĭsta. Spasibo.*

Эмили: Пожалуйста.
Ėmili: *Pozhaluĭsta.*

Триша: Вы не против, если мы остановимся у книжного магазина Стрэнд по дороге в кино?
Trisha: *Vy ne protiv, esli my ostanovimsi͡a u knizhnogo magazina Strėnd po doroge v kino?*

Эмили: Нет, конечно.
Ėmili: *Net, konechno.*

Майра: Я слышала, что у них появились новые книги, поэтому я хотела бы зайти и посмотреть.
Maĭra: *I͡A slyshala, chto u nikh poi͡avilis' novye knigi, poėtomu i͡a khotela by zaĭti i posmotret'.*

Триша: Я заказала слишком много еды. Кто-нибудь хочет попробовать мою еду?
Trisha: $\widehat{IA}$ *zakazala slishkom mnogo edy. Kto-nibud' khochet poprobovat' mo*$\widehat{iu}$ *edu?*

Эмили: Да, дай мне немного. Выглядит вкусно.
Émili: *Da, da*$\widehat{i}$ *mne nemnogo. Vygl*$\widehat{ia}$*dit vkusno.*

Триша: А ты, Майра?
Trisha: *A ty, Ma*$\widehat{i}$*ra?*

Майра: Нет, спасибо. У меня уже достаточно еды.
Ma$\widehat{i}$*ra:* *Net, spasibo. U men*$\widehat{ia}$ *uzhe dostatochno edy.*

Эмили: Триша, не хочешь попробовать одну мою фахиту?
Émili: *Trisha, ne khochesh' poprobovat' odnu mo*$\widehat{iu}$ *fakhitu?*

Триша: Да, хочу.
Trisha: *Da, khochu.*

Эмили: Ну вот. Хочешь другую попробовать?
Émili: *Nu vot. Xochesh' drugu*$\widehat{iu}$ *poprobovat'?*

Триша: О, этого более чем достаточно! Спасибо.
Trisha: *O, étogo bolee chem dostatochno! Spasibo.*

Майра: Ну, я думаю, мы все поели? Теперь нам надо уходить, чтобы не попасть в трафик; иначе мы опоздаем.
Ma$\widehat{i}$*ra:* *Nu,* $\widehat{ia}$ *duma*$\widehat{iu}$*, my vse poeli? Teper' nam nado ukhodit', chtoby ne popast' v trafik; inache my opozdaem.*

Триша: Я готова идти, когда все будут готовы.
Trisha: $\widehat{IA}$ *gotova idti, kogda vse budut gotovy.*

Эмили: Я тоже. Пойдем.
Émili: $\widehat{IA}$ *tozhe. Po*$\widehat{i}$*dem.*

LUNCHTIME

Emily: Tricia, May I borrow your cell phone to call my mother after lunch?

Tricia: Yes, of course, Emily. Don't forget to tell her we said hello.

Maira: Emily, could you pass the pepper, please?

Emily: Certainly, here you are.

Maira: And the salt too, please. Thank you.

Emily: You're welcome.

Tricia: Would either of you mind if we stop by Strand Bookstore on the way to the movie?

Emily: No, not at all.

Maira: I heard they have a new book selection so I would love to stop by and check it out.

Tricia: I ordered too much food. Would anybody care to try some of my food?

Emily: Yes, I would like some. It looks delicious.

Tricia: How about you, Maira?

Maira: No, thank you. I have enough food already.

Emily: Tricia, would you like to taste one of my fajitas?

Tricia: Yes, please.

Emily: Here you go. Do you want another?

Tricia: Oh, that is more than enough! Thank you.

Maira: I imagine we are all finished eating? We should leave now to avoid the traffic; otherwise we will be late.

Tricia: I am ready to leave whenever you all are.

Emily: So am I. Let's go.

42. Поиск работы – POISK RABOTY
SEARCHING FOR A JOB

Матильда: Привет, Паоло, рада тебя видеть.
Matil'da: Privet, Paolo, rada tebi͡a videt'.

Паоло: И я, Матильда. Прошло много времени с тех пор, как я в последний раз видел тебя.
Paolo: I i͡a, Matil'da. Proshlo mnogo vremeni s tekh por, kak i͡a v posledni͡i raz videl tebi͡a.

Матильда: Да, в последний раз мы виделись на Хэллоуин. Как все?
Matil'da: Da, v posledni͡i raz my videlis' na Xélouin. Kak vse?

Паоло: У меня все хорошо. Было бы лучше, если бы я нашел себе новую работу.
Paolo: U meni͡a vse khorosho. Bylo by luchshe, esli by i͡a nashel sebe novui͡u rabotu.

Матильда: Почему ты ищешь новую работу?
Matil'da: Pochemu ty ishchesh' novui͡u rabotu?

Паоло: Ну, я закончил учебу на прошлой неделе. Теперь я хочу получить работу в области финансов.
Paolo: Nu, i͡a zakonchil uchebu na proshlo͡i nedele. Teper' i͡a khochu poluchit' rabotu v oblasti finansov.

Матильда: Ты давно ищешь новую работу?
Matil'da: Ty davno ishchesh' novui͡u rabotu?

Паоло: Только начал на этой неделе.
Paolo: Tol'ko nachal na éto͡i nedele.

Матильда: У тебя уже готовое резюме есть, верно?
Matil'da: U tebi͡a uzhe gotovoe rezi͡ume est', verno?

Паоло: Да.
Paolo: Da.

Матильда: Я бы тогда не волновалась. У тебя много амбиций, и я знаю, что ты вложишь всю свою энергию в то, чтобы получить то, что ты хочешь. Кроме того, рынок труда действительно хорош сейчас, и всем компаниям нужны финансовые аналитики.
Matil'da: I͡A by togda ne volnovalas'. U tebi͡a mnogo ambit͡siĭ, i i͡a znai͡u, chto ty vlozhish' vsi͡u svoi͡u ėnergii͡u v to, chtoby poluchit' to, chto ty khochesh'. Krome togo, rynok truda deĭstvitel'no khorosh seĭchas, i vsem kompanii͡am nuzhny finansovye analitiki.

Паоло: Я надеюсь на это. Спасибо за совет.
Paolo: I͡A nadei͡us' na ėto. Spasibo za sovet.

SEARCHING FOR A JOB

Matilda: Hi Paolo, it is good to see you.

Paolo: Same here, Matilda. It has been a long time since I last saw you.

Matilda: Yes, the last time we saw each other was around Halloween. How is everything?

Paolo: I am doing OK. It would be better if I had a new job.

Matilda: Why are looking for a new job?

Paolo: Well, I graduated last week. Now, I want to get a job in the Finance field.

Matilda: Have you been looking for a new job for a while?

Paolo: I just started this week.

Matilda: You have prepared a resume, right?

Paolo: Yes.

Matilda: I wouldn't worry then. You have a lot of ambition and I know you will put all of your energy into getting what you want. Besides, the job market is really good right now, and all companies need financial analysts.

Paolo: I hope so. Thank you for the advice.

43. Собеседование на работу – sobesedovanie na rabotu Job Interview

Хью: Здравствуйте, Зак. Давайте начнем интервью. Вы готовы?
X'iu: Zdravstvuĭte, Zak. Davaĭte nachnem interv'iu. Vy gotovy?

Зак: Да, готов.
Zak: Da, gotov.

Хью: Отлично. Прежде всего, позвольте мне представиться. Я менеджер компании по логистике. Мне нужно как можно скорее найти человека на позицию начального уровня.
X'iu: Otlichno. Prezhde vsego, pozvol'te mne predstavit'sia. IA menedzher kompanii po logistike. Mne nuzhno kak mozhno skoree naĭti cheloveka na pozitsiiu nachal'nogo urovnia.

Зак: Замечательно. Не могли бы вы рассказать мне немного о позиции и ваших ожиданиях?
Zak: Zamechatel'no. Ne mogli by vy rasskazat' mne nemnogo o pozitsii i vashikh ozhidaniiakh?

Хью: Новому сотруднику придется тесно сотрудничать с производственным отделом. Существует также требование работа с банком на ежедневной основе.
X'iu: Novomu sotrudniku pridetsia tesno sotrudnichat' s proizvodstvennym otdelom. Sushchestvuet takzhe trebovanie rabota s bankom na ezhednevnoĭ osnove.

Зак: Какая квалификация вам нужна?
Zak: Kakaia kvalifikatsiia vam nuzhna?

Хью: Мне нужно четырехлетнее высшее образование в области делового администрирования. Некоторый предыдущий опыт работы будет полезен.

X'i͡u: Mne nuzhno chetyrekhletnee vysshee obrazovanie v oblasti delovogo administrirovanii͡a. Nekotoryĭ predydushchiĭ opyt raboty budet polezen.

Зак: Какой опыт нужен?

Zak: Kakoĭ opyt nuzhen?

Хью: Общая офисная работа подойдет. Я не требую большого опыта. На рабочем месте будет предоставлено обучение для нужного человека.

X'i͡u: Obshchai͡a ofisnai͡a rabota podoĭdet. I͡A ne trebui͡u bol'shogo opyta. Na rabochem meste budet predostavleno obuchenie dli͡a nuzhnogo cheloveka.

Зак: Это здорово!

Zak: Ėto zdorovo!

Хью: Каковы ваши сильные стороны? Почему я должен нанять вас?

X'i͡u: Kakovy vashi sil'nye storony? Pochemu i͡a dolzhen nani͡at' vas?

Зак: Я трудолюбивый человек и быстро учусь. Я очень хочу учиться, и я прекрасно умею ладить со всеми.

Zak: I͡A trudoli͡ubivyĭ chelovek i bystro uchus'. I͡A ochen' khochu uchit'si͡a, i i͡a prekrasno umei͡u ladit' so vsemi.

Хью: Хорошо. Вы не против работать долгие часы?

X'i͡u: Xorosho. Vy ne protiv rabotat' dolgie chasy?

Зак: Нет, я совсем не против.

Zak: Net, i͡a sovsem ne protiv.

Хью: Вы можете справиться с напряжением?
X'i͡u: Vy mozhete spravit'si͡a s napri͡azheniem?

Зак: Да. Когда я ходил в школу, у меня было 5 курсов каждый семестр, работ, как минимум, двадцать пять часов в неделю.
Zak: Da. Kogda i͡a khodil v shkolu, u meni͡a bylo 5 kursov kazhdyĭ semestr, rabot, kak minimum, dvadt͡sat' pi͡at' chasov v nedeli͡u.

Хью: У вас есть вопросы ко мне в данный момент?
X'i͡u: U vas est' voprosy ko mne v dannyĭ moment?

Зак: Нет, я думаю, что мне все понятно по работе.
Zak: Net, i͡a dumai͡u, chto mne vse poni͡atno po rabote.

Хью: Хорошо, Зак, было приятно познакомиться. Спасибо, что пришли.
X'i͡u: Xorosho, Zak, bylo pri͡atno poznakomit'si͡a. Spasibo, chto prishli.

Зак: Приятно было познакомиться. Спасибо, что встретились со мной.
Zak: Pri͡atno bylo poznakomit'si͡a. Spasibo, chto vstretilis' so mnoĭ.

JOB INTERVIEW

Hugh: Welcome Zach. Let's start the interview. Are you ready?

Zach: Yes, I am.

Hugh: Great. First of all, let me properly introduce myself. I am the company Logistics Manager. I need to fill an entry-level position as soon as possible.

Zach: Wonderful. Could you tell me a little bit about the position and your expectations?

Hugh: The new employee will have to work closely with the manufacturing department. There is also a requirement to deal with the bank on a daily basis.

Zach: What type of qualifications do you require?

Hugh: I require a four-year college degree in business administration. Some previous work experience would be helpful.

Zach: What kind of experience are you looking for?

Hugh: General office work is fine. I do not require a lot of experience. There will be on the job training for the right person.

Zach: That is great!

Hugh: What are your strengths? Why should I hire you?

Zach: I am a hard-working person and a fast learner. I am very eager to learn, and I get along fine with everyone.

Hugh: Alright. You do not mind working long hours, do you?

Zach: No, I do not mind at all.

Hugh: Can you handle pressure?

Zach: Yes. When I was going to school, I took 5 courses each semester while working at least twenty-five hours every week.

Hugh: Do you have any questions for me at this time?

Zach: No, I think I have a pretty good understanding of the job.

Hugh: Ok, Zach it was nice meeting you. Thank you for coming.

Zach: Nice meeting you too. Thank you for seeing me.

44. ДАЕМ ПРЕЗЕНТАЦИЮ – DAEM PREZENTAT͡SII͡U
GIVING A PRESENTATION

Салли: Мне нужно будет выступить с докладом о глобальном потеплении в пятницу, и я так нервничаю.
Salli: Mne nuzhno budet vystupit' s dokladom o global'nom poteplenii v pi͡atnit͡su, i i͡a tak nervnichai͡u.

Ольга: Есть много способов, которые помогут чувствовать себя более уверенно и меньше нервничать.
Ol'ga: Est' mnogo sposobov, kotorye pomogut chuvstvovat' sebi͡a bolee uverenno i men'she nervnichat'.

Салли: Что мне делать, Ольга?
Salli: CHto mne delat', Ol'ga?

Ольга: Вы провели исследование по этой теме?
Ol'ga: Vy proveli issledovanie po éto͡ĭ teme?

Салли: На самом деле я провела много исследований по этому вопросу, и я знаю, что могу ответить практически на любые вопросы, которые я получу от аудитории.
Salli: Na samom dele i͡a provela mnogo issledovani͡ĭ po étomu voprosu, i i͡a znai͡u, chto mogu otvetit' prakticheski na li͡ubye voprosy, kotorye i͡a poluchu ot auditorii.

Ольга: Обязательно создайте набросок своей презентации.
Ol'ga: Obi͡azatel'no sozda͡ĭte nabrosok svoe͡ĭ prezentat͡sii.

Салли: Вы правы. Это поможет мне организовать всю информацию.
Salli: Vy pravy. Éto pomozhet mne organizovat' vsi͡u informat͡sii͡u.

125

Ольга: Да. Это поможет вам понять, что должно быть представлено во-первых, во-вторых, в-третьих ...
Ol'ga: Da. Ėto pomozhet vam poniȃt', chto dolzhno byt' predstavleno vo-pervykh, vo-vtorykh, v-tret'ikh ...

Ольга: Хорошая идея! Важно иметь факты в поддержку вашей презентации. Вы хотите, чтобы презентация была убедительной.
Ol'ga: Xoroshaiȃ ideiȃ! Vazhno imet' fakty v podderzhku vasheĭ prezentat͡sii. Vy khotite, chtoby prezentat͡siiȃ byla ubeditel'noĭ.

Салли: Я собираюсь сделать это прямо сейчас! Спасибо.
Salli: IȂ sobiraiȗs' sdelat' ėto priȃmo seĭchas! Spasibo.

Ольга: У вас будет отличная презентация.
Ol'ga: U vas budet otlichnaiȃ prezentat͡siiȃ.

GIVING A PRESENTATION

Sally: I will have to give a presentation on global warming on Friday, and I am so nervous.

Olga: There are a lot of things you can do to make you feel more confident and less nervous.

Sally: What should I do, Olga?

Olga: Have you done your research on the topic?

Sally: In fact, I have done a lot of research on the subject, and I know I can answer almost any questions I will receive from the audience.

Olga: Make sure to create an outline of your presentation.

Sally: You're right. This will help me organize all of the information.

Olga: Yes. It will help you figure out what should present first, second, third...

Olga: Good idea! It is important to have facts to support your presentation. You want the presentation to be credible.

Sally: I'm going to do that right now! Thank you.

Olga: You're going to have a great presentation.

45. Окончание школы – Okonchanie shkoly
GRADUATION

Лиз: Чудесный букет цветов. Для кого это?
Liz: CHudesnyĭ buket t͡svetov. Dli͡a kogo éto?

Энни: Эти цветы для моей сестры Сильвии. Она заканчивает сегодня университет.
Énni: Éti t͡svety dli͡a moeĭ sestry Sil'vii. Ona zakanchivaet segodni͡a universitet.

Лиз: Эти цветы, наверное, стоили тебе целое состояние.
Liz: Éti t͡svety, navernoe, stoili tebe t͡seloe sostoi͡anie.

Энни: Я заплатила за них семьдесят долларов.
Énni: I͡A zaplatila za nikh sem'desi͡at dollarov.

Лиз: Это довольно дорого.
Liz: Éto dovol'no dorogo.

Энни: Моя сестра работала очень много последние четыре года, чтобы получить диплом. Для меня трата этой суммы денег того стоит.
Énni: Moi͡a sestra rabotala ochen' mnogo poslednie chetyre goda, chtoby poluchit' diplom. Dli͡a meni͡a trata étoĭ summy deneg togo stoit.

Лиз: Это очень мило с твоей стороны. Я хотела бы, чтобы и мы заканчивали сегодня. Это так захватывающе!
Liz: Éto ochen' milo s tvoeĭ storony. I͡A khotela by, chtoby i my zakanchivali segodni͡a. Éto tak zakhvatyvai͡ushche!

Энни: Только нам еще три года, и мы тоже закончим. Мы закончим очень быстро, не успеем оглянуться. Время летит очень быстро.
Énni: Tol'ko nam eshche tri goda, i my tozhe zakonchim. My zakonchim ochen' bystro, ne uspeem ogli͡anut'si͡a. Vremi͡a letit ochen' bystro.

GRADUATION

Liz: That is a wonderful bouquet of flowers. Who is it for?

Annie: These flowers are for my sister Silvia. She is graduating today.

Liz: It must have cost you a fortune.

Annie: I paid seventy dollars for them.

Liz: That is quite expensive.

Annie: My sister worked very the last four years for her degree. To me spending that amount of money is worth it.

Liz: That is very nice of you. I wish we were graduating today. This is so exciting!

Annie: We only have another three years and we will be done also. We'll be graduating before we realize it. Time goes by very fast.

46. Хэллоуин – Xẻllouin

HALLOWEEN

Эли: Ты веришь, что завтра уже Хэллоуин, Эллисон? Время летит так быстро! Сегодня 30 октября! Ты уже решила, какой костюм наденешь?
Ẻli: Ty verish', chto zavtra uzhe Xẻllouin, Ẻllison? Vremi͡a letit tak bystro! Segodni͡a 30 okti͡abri͡a! Ty uzhe reshila, kakoĭ kosti͡um nadenesh'?

Эллисон: Я все еще не определилась. Я хочу надеть костюм тостера или костюм гангстера-рэпера. Мне всегда было интересно, почему есть традиция так наряжаться на Хэллоуин.
Ẻllison: I͡A vse eshche ne opredelilas'. I͡A khochu nadet' kosti͡um tostera ili kosti͡um gangstera-rẻpera. Mne vsegda bylo interesno, pochemu est' tradi͡tsii͡a tak nari͡azhat'si͡a na Xẻllouin.

Эли: Это делает празднование намного веселее!
Ẻli: Ẻto delaet prazdnovanie namnogo veselee!

Эллисон: Да, я помню, как мы много веселились в прошлом году, когда мама взяла меня с собой в костюме кошки. Ты знаешь, кем хочешь быть, Эли?
Ẻllison: Da, i͡a pomni͡u, kak my mnogo veselilis' v proshlom godu, kogda mama vzi͡ala meni͡a s soboĭ v kosti͡ume koshki. Ty znaesh', kem khochesh' byt', Ẻli?

Эли: Я хочу быть бурундуком!
Ẻli: I͡A khochu byt' burundukom!

Эллисон: Отличная идея!
Ẻllison: Otlichnai͡a idei͡a!

Эли: Отлично! Тогда, ты будешь гангстером рэпером, а я - бурундуком. Пойдем, спросим маму, можем ли мы пойти завтра вечером самостоятельно ходить выпрашивать сладости.
Éli: Otlichno! Togda, ty budesh' gangsterom réperom, a i͡a - burundukom. Poĭdem, sprosim mamu, mozhem li my poĭti zavtra vecherom samostoi͡atel'no khodit' vyprashivat' sladosti.

Эллисон: Хорошо, пойдем, спросим маму!
Éllison: Xorosho, poĭdem, sprosim mamu!

HALLOWEEN

Eli: Can you believe that tomorrow is Halloween Allison? Time goes by so fast! Today is October 30th! Have you already decided what costume you want to wear?

Allison: I'm still undecided. I want to wear either a toaster costume or a gangster rapper costume. I have always wondered why it's a tradition to dress up for Halloween.

Eli: Dressing up makes celebrating the holiday much more fun!

Allison: Yes, I remember having a lot of fun last year when mom took me around in a cat outfit. Do you know what you want to be yet, Eli?

Eli: I want to be a chipmunk!

Allison: That's a great idea!

Eli: Great! So you will be a gangster rapper and I will be a chipmunk. Let's go ask mom if we can go trick-or-treating tomorrow night by ourselves.

Allison: Ok, let's go ask mom!

47. В ГОСТИНИЦЕ - V GOSTINITSE
AT A HOTEL

Администратор отеля: Добрый вечер.
Administrator otelia̅: Dobryĭ vecher.

Эли: Добрый вечер. Мы с женой хотели бы комнату на одну ночь, пожалуйста. Случайно у вас нет номера в наличии?
Éli: Dobryĭ vecher. My s zhenoĭ khoteli by komnatu na odnu noch', pozhaluĭsta. Sluchaĭno u vas net nomera v nalichii?

Администратор отеля: Есть ли у вас бронирование?
Administrator otelia̅: Est' li u vas bronirovanie?

Эли: К сожалению, у нас нет бронирования.
Éli: K sozhalenii̅u, u nas net bronirovanii̅a.

Администратор отеля: ОК. Дайте я проверю и посмотрю, что у нас есть. Похоже, вам повезло. У нас осталась только одна комната.
Administrator otelia̅: OK. Daĭte i̅a proveri̅u i posmotri̅u, chto u nas est'. Pokhozhe, vam povezlo. U nas ostalas' tol'ko odna komnata.

Эли: Отлично. Мы ехали весь день и очень устали. Нам просто нужно место для отдыха на всю ночь.
Éli: Otlichno. My ekhali ves' den' i ochen' ustali. Nam prosto nuzhno mesto dli̅a otdykha na vsi̅u noch'.

Администратор отеля: В этом номере все будет хорошо. Это уютная комната с двуспальной кроватью и полностью оборудованной кухней.
Administrator otelia̅: V étom nomere vse budet khorosho. Éto ui̅utnai̅a komnata s dvuspal'noĭ krovat'i̅u i polnost'i̅u oborudovannoĭ kukhneĭ.

Эли: Сколько стоит ночь?
Éli: Skol'ko stoit noch'?

Администратор отеля: 179 долларов за ночь. Кто-нибудь еще будет в номере с вами?
Administrator otelía: 179 dollarov za noch'. Kto-nibud' eshche budet v nomere s vami?

Эли: Нас только двое. Я знаю, что уже поздно, но есть ли поблизости ресторан?
Éli: Nas tol'ko dvoe. ÍA znaíu, chto uzhe pozdno, no est' li poblizosti restoran?

Администратор отеля: В отеле есть ресторан, будет открыт еще час. Вы хотите оплатить номер кредитной картой?
Administrator otelía: V otele est' restoran, budet otkryt eshche chas. Vy khotite oplatit' nomer kreditnoǐ kartoǐ?

Эли: Да. Вот, пожалуйста.
Éli: Da. Vot, pozhaluǐsta.

Администратор отеля: Спасибо. Для вас все готово. Наслаждайтесь отдыхом.
Administrator otelía: Spasibo. Dlía vas vse gotovo. Naslazhdaǐtes' otdykhom.

AT A HOTEL

Hotel Receptionist: Good evening.

Eli: Hello, good evening. My wife and I need a room for the night please. By chance do you have one available?

Hotel Receptionist: Do you have a reservation?

Eli: Unfortunately, we do not have a reservation.

Hotel Receptionist: Ok. Let me check and see what we have. It looks you're in luck. We have only one room left.

Eli: Excellent. We have been driving all day and we're very tired. We just need a place to relax for the rest of the night.

Hotel Receptionist: This room should do just fine then. It is a cozy room with a king size bed and full kitchen.

Eli: How much is it for the night?

Hotel Receptionist: It's $179 for the room. Is there anyone else staying in the room with you?

Eli: It's just the two of us. I know that it's late at night, but is there any restaurant open nearby?

Hotel Receptionist: There's a restaurant open for another hour in the hotel. Do you want to pay for the room with a credit card?

Eli: Yes. Here you go.

Hotel Receptionist: Thank you. You're all set. Enjoy the rest of the night.

48. Студент из-за рубежа – Student iz-za rubezha
A Foreign Student

Дрю: Здравствуйте, вы миссис Макнамара?
Dri͡u: Zdravstvuĭte, vy missis Maknamara?

Миссис Макнамара: Да, это я. Вы должны быть Дрю. Мы ждали вас.
Missis Maknamara: Da, éto i͡a. Vy dolzhny byt' Dri͡u. My zhdali vas.

Дрю: Я должна была прибыть два дня назад, но мой рейс из Колумбии был перенесен.
Dri͡u: I͡A dolzhna byla pribyt' dva dni͡a nazad, no moĭ reĭs iz Kolumbii byl perenesen.

Миссис Макнамара: Хорошо, я рада, что вы долетели безопасно, вот что наиболее важно. Хотите чаю?
Missis Maknamara: Xorosho, i͡a rada, chto vy doleteli bezopasno, vot chto naibolee vazhno. Xotite chai͡u?

Дрю: Я бы с удовольствием, если вам не сложно. У вас красивый дом.
Dri͡u: I͡A by s udovol'stviem, esli vam ne slozhno. U vas krasivyĭ dom.

Миссис Макнамара: Спасибо. Мы переехали в Калифорнию из Колумбии пять лет назад и решили купить этот дом. Мы очень любим его.
Missis Maknamara: Spasibo. My pereekhali v Kaliforni͡iu iz Kolumbii pi͡at' let nazad i reshili kupit' étot dom. My ochen' li͡ubim ego.

Дрю: Я привезла вам подарок.
Dri͡u: I͡A privezla vam podarok.

Миссис Макнамара: Ой, не нужно было. Какое красивое ожерелье. Спасибо. Как долго вы будете здесь?
Missis Maknamara: Oĭ, ne nuzhno bylo. Kakoe krasivoe ozherel'e. Spasibo. Kak dolgo vy budete zdes'?

Дрю: Не за что. Я планирую остаться в Калифорнии на пять месяцев, чтобы практиковать свой английский. Я действительно волнуюсь, как я пойду в английскую школу и буду там учиться.
Drĭu: Ne za chto. I͡A planirui͡u ostat'si͡a v Kalifornii na pi͡at' mesi͡at͡sev, chtoby praktikovat' svoĭ angliĭskiĭ. I͡A deĭstvitel'no volnui͡us', kak i͡a poĭdu v angliĭskui͡u shkolu i budu tam uchit'si͡a.

Миссис Макнамара: Хорошо, я покажу вам вашу комнату, и вы можете отдохнуть. Вы, должно быть, устали от всех этих поездок.
Missis Maknamara: Xorosho, i͡a pokazhu vam vashu komnatu, i vy mozhete otdokhnut'. Vy, dolzhno byt', ustali ot vsekh étikh poezdok.

A FOREIGN STUDENT

Drew: Hello, are you Mrs. McNamara?

Mrs. McNamara: Yes, I am. You must be Drew. We have been expecting you.

Drew: I was supposed to arrive two days ago, but my flight out of Colombia was delayed.

Mrs. McNamara: Well, I'm glad that you made it safely, that's is what is most important. Would you like some tea?

Drew: I would love some, if it's not too much trouble. You have a beautiful home.

Mrs. McNamara: Thank you. We moved to California from Colombia five years ago and decided to buy this house. We absolutely love it.

Drew: I brought you a gift.

Mrs. McNamara: Oh, you shouldn't have. This is a beautiful necklace. Thank you. How long will you be here for?

Drew: You're welcome. I plan to stay in California for five months to practice speaking English. I am really excited to go to the English school and learn.

Mrs. McNamara: Well, let me show you your room and you can relax. You must be tired from all of the traveling.

49. Промедление – PROMEDLENIE
PROCRASTINATION

Скотти: Ты уже написала свой исследовательский отчет? Его нужно сдать через две недели.
Skotti: Ty uzhe napisala svoĭ issledovatel'skiĭ otchet? Ego nuzhno sdat' cherez dve nedeli.

Мередит: Нет, я еще не начала работать над ним. У меня достаточно времени, чтобы сделать это на следующей неделе.
Meredit: Net, ĩa eshche ne nachala rabotat' nad nim. U menĩa dostatochno vremeni, chtoby sdelat' éto na sleduĩushcheĭ nedele.

Скотти: Я точно помню, что ты говорила на прошлой и предыдущей неделе. Так как у тебя так много свободного времени во время отпуска, ты должна сделать это.
Skotti: ĨA tochno pomnĩu, chto ty govorila na proshloĭ i predydushcheĭ nedele. Tak kak u tebĩa tak mnogo svobodnogo vremeni vo vremĩa otpuska, ty dolzhna sdelat' éto.

Мередит: Проблема в том, что мне сложно с этим предметом, и я думаю, что мне, возможно, понадобится помощь. Иначе я могу подвести весь класс.
Meredit: Problema v tom, chto mne slozhno s étim predmetom, i ĩa dumaĩu, chto mne, vozmozhno, ponadobitsĩa pomoshch'. Inache ĩa mogu podvesti ves' klass.

Скотти: У меня есть решение. Перестань думать о помощи и найди репетитора.
Skotti: U menĩa est' reshenie. Perestan' dumat' o pomoshchi i naĭdi repetitora.

Мередит: Ты права. Мне нужно быть проактивной и искать помощь. Я начинаю искать завтра.
Meredit: *Ty prava. Mne nuzhno byt' proaktivnoĭ i iskat' pomoshch'. ĨA nachinaĩu iskat' zavtra.*

Скотти: Завтра? Нет, ты должна найти ее сегодня!
Skotti: *Zavtra? Net, ty dolzhna naĭti ee segodnĩa!*

Мередит: Я знаю, я просто шучу. Я сделаю это сегодня.
Meredit: *ĨA znaĩu, ĩa prosto shuchu. ĨA sdelaĩu éto segodnĩa.*

PROCRASTINATION

Scottie: Have you written your research report yet? It's due in two weeks.

Meredith: No, I haven't started working on it yet. I have plenty of time to do it next week though.

Scottie: I distinctly remember that's what you said last week and the week before that. Since you have so much free time during the holiday you should get it done.

Meredith: The problem is that I am struggling in that class and I think I might need to get a tutor. Otherwise I might fail the entire class.

Scottie: I have a solution. Stop thinking about getting help and get a tutor.

Meredith: You're right. I need to be proactive and get help. I start looking tomorrow.

Scottie: Tomorrow? No, you have to find one today!

Meredith: I know, I'm just kidding. I will do it today.

50. ГДЕ МОЙ БРАТ? - GDE MOĬ BRAT?
WHERE'S MY BROTHER

Карисса: Я не могу найти своего младшего брата, Даниэля. Я думала, что он шел прямо позади меня, и теперь он пропал. Пожалуйста, помогите мне.
Karissa: ĨA ne mogu naĭti svoego mladshego brata, Daniélĩa. ĨA dumala, chto on shel prĩamo pozadi menĩa, i teper' on propal. Pozhaluĭsta, pomogite mne.

Полицейский: Он, наверное, потерялся в толпе. Сейчас много людей делают покупки к праздникам. Во что он одет?
Politseĭskiĭ: On, navernoe, poterĩalsĩa v tolpe. Seĭchas mnogo lĩudeĭ delaĩut pokupki k prazdnikam. Vo chto on odet?

Карисса: На нем синий пиджак и черные шорты. Ему всего 5 лет.
Karissa: Na nem siniĭ pidzhak i chernye shorty. Emu vsego 5 let.

Полицейский: Кажется, я видел его в раздевалке. Дай мне проверить. У него светлые волосы?
Politseĭskiĭ: Kazhetsĩa, ĩa videl ego v razdevalke. Daĭ mne proverit'. U nego svetlye volosy?

Карисса: Да. Вы нашли его?
Karissa: Da. Vy nashli ego?

Полицейский: Нет, это был не он. Давай проверим магазин игрушек здесь рядом.
Politseĭskiĭ: Net, éto byl ne on. Davaĭ proverim magazin igrushek zdes' rĩadom.

Карисса: Он любит играть с Лего, я должна была подумать об этом!
Karissa: On lîubit igrat' s Lego, îa dolzhna byla podumat' ob ėtom!

Полицейский: Я вижу много детей повсюду. Там есть твой брат?
Politseĭskiĭ: ÎA vizhu mnogo deteĭ povsîudu. Tam est' tvoĭ brat?

Карисса: Даниэль! Ну вот, Дэниэль, не теряйся опять! Ты напугал меня до смерти!
Karissa: Daniėl'! Nu vot, Dėniėl', ne terîaĭsîa opîat'! Ty napugal menîa do smerti!

Полицейский: Пожалуйста, следите за ним, чтобы это больше не повторилось. Здесь может быть опасно ходить самостоятельно.
Politseĭskiĭ: Pozhaluĭsta, sledite za nim, chtoby ėto bol'she ne povtorilos'. Zdes' mozhet byt' opasno khodit' samostoîatel'no.

Карисса: Вы правы. Я буду лучше следить за ним.
Karissa: Vy pravy. ÎA budu luchshe sledit' za nim.

Полицейский: Хорошо. А теперь иди и найди своих родителей и хорошего дня.
Politseĭskiĭ: Xorosho. A teper' idi i naĭdi svoikh roditeleĭ i khoroshego dnîa.

Карисса: Спасибо, офицер, за вашу помощь.
Karissa: Spasibo, ofîtser, za vashu pomoshch'.

WHERE'S MY BROTHER

Carissa: I can't find my little brother, Daniel. I thought he was right behind me and now he's missing. Please help me.

Police officer: He probably got lost in the crowd. There are a lot of people shopping for the holidays. What kind of clothes is he wearing?

Carissa: He has a blue jacket and black shorts. He's only 5 years old.

Police officer: I think I saw him go into the dressing room. Let me check. Does he have blonde hair?

Carissa: Yes. Did you find him?

Police officer: No, that was not him. Let's check the toy store next door.

Carissa: He loves playing with Legos, I should have thought of that!

Police officer: I see a lot of children everywhere. Are any of them your brother?

Carissa: Daniel! There you are, don't you wander off like that again! You scared me to death!

Police officer: Please keep an eye on him so that this doesn't happen again. It can be dangerous wandering around all by himself.

Carissa: You're right. I will take better care of watching him.

Police officer: Alright. Now go find your parents and have a good day.

Carissa: Thank you officer for all of your help.

Conclusion

Well reader, we hope that you found these dual language dialogues helpful. Remember that the best way to learn this material is through repetition, memorization and conversation.

We encourage you to review the dialogues again, find a friend and practice your Russian by role playing. Not only will you have more fun doing it this way, but you will find that you will remember even more!

Keep in mind, that every day you practice, the closer you will get to speaking fluently.

You can expect many more books from us, so keep your eyes peeled. Thank you again for reading our book and we look forward to seeing you again.

About the Author

Touri is an innovative language education brand that is disrupting the way we learn languages. Touri has a mission to make sure language learning is not just easier but engaging and a ton of fun.

Besides the excellent books that they create, Touri also has an active website, which offers live fun and immersive 1-on-1 online language lessons with native instructors at nearly anytime of the day.

Additionally, Touri provides the best tips to improving your memory retention, confidence while speaking and fast track your progress on your journey to fluency.

Check out https://touri.co for more information.

OTHER BOOKS BY TOURI

SPANISH

Conversational Spanish Dialogues: 50 Spanish Conversations and Short Stories

Spanish Short Stories (Volume 1): 10 Exciting Short Stories to Easily Learn Spanish & Improve Your Vocabulary

Spanish Short Stories (Volume 2): 10 Exciting Short Stories to Easily Learn Spanish & Improve Your Vocabulary

Intermediate Spanish Short Stories (Volume 1): 10 Amazing Short Tales to Learn Spanish & Quickly Grow Your Vocabulary the Fun Way!

Intermediate Spanish Short Stories (Volume 2): 10 Amazing Short Tales to Learn Spanish & Quickly Grow Your Vocabulary the Fun Way!

100 Days of Real World Spanish: Useful Words & Phrases for All Levels to Help You Become Fluent Faster

100 Day Medical Spanish Challenge: Daily List of Relevant Medical Spanish Words & Phrases to Help You Become Fluent

FRENCH

Conversational French Dialogues: 50 French Conversations and Short Stories

French Short Stories for Beginners (Volume 1): 10 Exciting Short Stories to Easily Learn French & Improve Your Vocabulary

French Short Stories for Beginners (Volume 2): 10 Exciting Short Stories to Easily Learn French & Improve Your Vocabulary

Intermediate French Short Stories (Volume 1): 10 Amazing Short Tales to Learn French & Quickly Grow Your Vocabulary the Fun Way!

ITALIAN

Conversational Italian Dialogues: 50 Italian Conversations and Short Stories

PORTUGUESE

Conversational Portuguese Dialogues: 50 Portuguese Conversations and Short Stories

ARABIC

Conversational Arabic Dialogues: 50 Arabic Conversations and Short Stories

CHINESE

Conversational Chinese Dialogues: 50 Chinese Conversations and Short Stories

ONE LAST THING...

If you enjoyed this book or found it useful, we would be very grateful if you posted a short review on Amazon.

Your support really does make a difference and we read all the reviews personally. Your feedback will make this book even better.

Thanks again for your support!

9 781953 149183